OVER MY DEAD BODY

IVORY TOWER SPIES BOOK FIVE

EMILY KAZMIERSKI

Also by Emily Kazmierski

Ivory Tower Spies Series

For Your Ears Only
The Walk-in Agent (a Julep Short Story)
The Eyes of Spies
Spy Your Heart Out
Spy Got Your Tongue
Over My Dead Body

Other Novels

Malignant
Life Among the Ashes
All-American Liars

For all of you readers
who have been with me since my very first novel,
thank you. Your support means the world to me.

Chapter 1

"I'm sorry."

They're the last words Starling said before our comms went dead. Before the GPS signals in the watches Julep and Starling were wearing went dark.

What happened to them, exactly?

I run a hand through my hair, willing Royal to hurry up. It doesn't work. The houses on the tree-lined street slink by one by one, no faster than before. Royal isn't even speeding. It's like he's not even in a hurry.

"I'm trying not to attract attention," he says, eyeing me in the rearview mirror.

I clasp my hands in my lap to squash my apparently obvious fidgeting. "Can't you go a little faster?"

Finally he rounds a corner, and we're there. The street where CIA COO Gillian Harris lives is banded by immaculately kept homes standing proud in the sunlight. The few cars that remain in driveways along the road gleam. Crisply cut lawns of sparkling emerald green reach from the sidewalk up to the front doors of the homes, which are quiet in the middle of the day.

Clarity and Haru are huddled together in the row directly behind the driver's seat, petting Baron in long, smooth strokes.

The cat seems to have warmed to Clarity, but if anyone else gets near him, he emits an angry hiss, narrowing his vivid yellow eyes in warning. He's not here to make friends.

Lotus has been quiet the entire ride, brooding next to me in the back of Dr. Faraday's suburban, stealing nervous glances at Royal, who's up front in the driver's seat. Once, Lotus catches me watching him, and his eyes fall to his lap. But the jagged line of his lips doesn't change. I'm not the one being eaten alive by worry this time.

I almost wish I was.

Beside Royal, Truly sits prim and proper in the passenger seat, chatting casually, as if she wasn't spirited away in the night by a group of secret agents. Really, she's handling all of this remarkably well.

Royal inches Dr. Faraday's suburban forward, his eyes scanning for any sign of Charles Darnay or men from Cobalt Security.

A flash of light catches my eye, making me twist around toward it. Is it a gunman, crouched behind a car, waiting for us to spill out of the van so he can spill our blood in revenge for his fallen comrades?

My heart bobs in my throat as tension ripples through my limbs.

No. A child's bicycle lies deserted on the grass, coming into view as Royal pulls abreast of the property.

My body sags against the seat. I'm jumpy, my nerves raw. I inhale deeply, relaxing my muscles. Exhale a long breath slowly through my nose. And again.

"You knew? That Charles Darnay was Starling's dad?" Lotus's eyes are wary as he looks at me, and his words are coarse, like metal raked over coals.

Clarity swivels in her seat to meet my eyes, and Haru does

the same. One's look conveys sympathy, while the other, confusion.

A lump forms in my throat. "Yes," I push out. "I knew."

He bites the inside of his cheek, his eyes searching for something in my face. "Here I thought we were close, but come to find out you were keeping secrets, just like your dad."

I wince as his calculated barb pierces my heart. Is that what my entire team thinks of me? That I was withholding information? Shame washes over me, threatening to paint my face a vivid red. I push it down. "I can explain."

Lotus shakes his head, but I open my mouth to speak anyway. I need to set the record straight before any more time passes.

"We're here," Royal says in a low voice. He points ahead, to a large white house down the street. He pulls to the curb and cuts the engine.

I huff in frustration, but Lotus turns away from me, arms tight across his chest. I want to justify myself, but it will have to wait. I try to ignore the guilt coiling in my chest and focus on the street ahead.

The painter's van that Starling and Julep drove into the city is still parked under a spindly oak four houses down from where COO Harris lives. An unpaved road begins at the curb and winds between the homes in that direction. Where does it lead?

Royal catches Truly's eye for only a moment before twisting in his seat to face the rest of us. "Clarity, you're coming in with me. Are you ready?"

My sister gives a slow nod.

"I want to go, too," Lotus says, unbuckling his seatbelt and scooting forward.

My dad's lips purse as he studies the boy beside me.

A second stretches out, then another.

Royal gives a sturdy nod, and Lotus clenches a fist.

Haru retrieves earbuds from the small case at her feet and hands them out to each of us.

I activate mine and pop it into my ear.

With a sloppy swat, Lotus does the same.

Once Clarity's earbud is in place, her fingers unleash the buckle before going to the holster at her waist. Retrieving her gun with practiced hands, she rises to a crouch and rests her hand on the door handle. Her deep brown eyes meet mine, and there's no trace of her fear there—only grim determination.

Lotus, too, arms himself.

Royal slides out of his seat and waits for Clarity to climb out of the suburban, the sunlight cutting into the interior when the door swings open.

Baron hisses at this, and Haru quiets him with a low "Hush."

Lotus pushes the lever to release the seat, and pushes it forward to let himself out.

Reaching out, I put a hand on his back. "Good luck."

He glances back at me over his shoulder. "Thanks."

The three of them move over the street in lock-step, their precision honed and practiced from years of working together. They sneak along the sides of the painter's van and peer in the windows. "There's no sign of them in here," Clarity says as she moves in quiet grace.

"She's like a cat," Truly whispers from the front seat.

Baron seems to take umbrage at this, because he lifts his head and gives an angry yowl.

"Shh," Haru croons at the beast, stroking him on his arched back. Placated, the cat relaxes once more.

Royal, Clarity, and Lotus step up onto the grass and round

the far side of Harris's house out of sight.

My entire body aches to be with them, on the front lines of battle rather than here in what amounts to the medical tent. I've never been sidelined with an injury before, and the mantle of inadequacy settles around my neck. I shift in my seat, but it doesn't lessen the frustration.

My breathing is shallow as fear curls through me. What if my teammates find Julep laying on the cold cement in Gillian Harris's backyard, bleeding out? Or worse, already gone? My mouth goes dry and I lick my lips. I promised everyone that there wouldn't be any more loss, and I'm regretting that now. What a stupid thing to promise, especially in our line of work. Especially since I can only control my own actions, not the actions of every person I work with, or every person we come up against in the field.

"I'm sorry." Starling's words haunt me. They flicker in and out of the forefront of my mind, never far away.

"The side gate is still open," Royal says. "We're going in."

The hairs on the back of my neck rise to attention. "Be careful," I say, my voice closely controlled.

"We will," Clarity breathes in response.

The gate creaks through the comms, and a gasp sounds; it's my sister.

"What is it?" I ask, my heart beating in anxious anticipation. "Is someone... dead?" Please don't let it be Julep. Please. Please.

"There's some blood on the ground," Royal says in a matter-of-fact voice.

"Does it look like... a lot?" Haru asks, her voice a barely audible squeak.

"Not enough to worry about. Let's keep moving."

My shoulders sag in relief.

11

"The back door is open," my sister informs us. "We're going inside."

"Is it weird being on the outside looking in?" Haru asks, turning around in her seat to look at me.

"You have no idea." My mind recalls my team leaving for St. Petersburg those few months ago, leaving Haru and me alone in the Ivory Tower. The restlessness I felt then is nothing to the feeling of uselessness coursing through me now. The bullet wound in my thigh burns, and a tiny gasp escapes me. I shift my weight away from that leg. The tiny amount of painkillers I let Dr. Faraday give me must be wearing off.

"Why don't you put your leg up?" Truly asks, turning her bright, ocean-blue eyes toward me.

"I'm fine."

She gives me a knowing look, but doesn't push it. Instead, she turns back toward COO Harris's house, her fingers tangled in her lap.

My heart beats a worried rhythm in my chest as the silence stretches. What are my teammates going to find inside Harris's house? More blood? Or worse, bodies?

"The house is clear," Royal says. "There's no one here."

I lean my head back against the headrest and close my eyes. Julep is probably still alive. She's likely being held by Darnay, but she's alive. And Starling… He had everyone fooled.

"It looks like Ms. Harris put up quite a fight," Clarity adds. "There isn't a single piece of furniture that's in its rightful place, and her bedroom door has been kicked in. There's a Cobalt guy unconscious in here. Dad is restraining him now. The coast is clear, if you want to come inside."

She doesn't have to ask me twice.

There's a thin trail of blood leading from the back yard through the sun-dappled trees to an unpaved road that winds behind COO Harris's property. Fresh tire tracks in the dirt hint at the presence of a large vehicle, but that's the only trace left behind by Darnay's men.

I go still, following the trail back toward the house with scrutinizing eyes. I lean on my crutch, reaching up with my free hand to massage my scalp. It's itchy under my unwashed hair.

Beside me, Lotus stands, ashen face hardening in the morning light. "We have to get her back," he whispers.

I reach out to pat his arm, but he flinches away from me. I withdraw, clenching my fingers into a fist.

Clarity puts a reassuring hand on his arm, and he doesn't move. She shoots a glance toward me.

The rejection stings, but I can't blame him for it. Maybe I was keeping secrets, just like my dad. Maybe I've been made in his image, and doomed to repeat the same mistakes.

"We can't stay here," I say at last, and moving as quickly as I can despite my crutch, I lead my team toward the back of the house.

Even at this moment, Darnay and his men could be lurking nearby, waiting to attack. As long as we're here at COO Harris's house, we're in danger. We have to move to a secure location. Fast.

Chapter 2

Once we're all back in Dr. Faraday's suburban, my dad drives us to a big box store nearby and pulls into a secluded spot behind the store's hulking beige structure. It's strange working in the middle of the day like this, but we don't have a choice. The more time Darnay has hostages, the more chances there are for him to do them harm. The clock is ticking.

"It's logical to assume that Charles took Julep and Gillian Harris hostage, since there wasn't much blood at the scene," Royal says, summing up his findings.

"And Starling," I put in.

In the seat beside me, Lotus shifts, avoiding looking at my face, his jaw set.

Royal shoots me a look, but doesn't argue.

I push on. "The question is, where would he take them? Why not simply kill her like he did that other guy?"

"And why take Julep and Starling?" Haru asks. "Not that I'm not incredibly relieved."

"It's clear that he wants Royal to come after them," I put in, tapping my fingers on my uninjured thigh. "But where?"

The interior of the van falls silent, each of us wondering what Darnay's next move will be.

My eyes skim around the inside of the van, looking for inspiration.

Haru flips her laptop open, calls up an Internet window, and starts typing. "What about Julep's old employee login on Mr. Darnay's server? She mentioned it to me once. He uses it to send documents and information to his employees. Ha! Here it is."

Royal leans over his armrest to get a closer look.

Haru swivels the laptop so he can see the screen. "See?"

"How long do you think it'll take you to login to her account?"

"That's if he hasn't deleted her login information," Lotus grumbles.

"Julep told me that Charles wasn't thrilled when she resigned. Perhaps he didn't shut down her account, as a bit of wishful thinking," Royal says.

"That's kind of a stretch," I say, eyebrows cocked. "Even if he hadn't done it yet, there's no way he'd leave it open now that he knows what he knows… about you."

"This is going to take hours to crack," Haru moans.

My eyes rove over the bland beige structure before us. Unlike the Tower, it has no character, no interesting features. It's almost as boring as Darnay's hotels are embellished. I drop my gaze to my watch. "You can stop trying to get into Darnay's server. Think about it. Darnay is a famous hotelier with luxury properties all across Europe and Asia, right? But he doesn't have many holdings here in the US. I'm betting that if and when he purchased any land here, it'll have made headlines. Haru, can you do a news search for Darnay's holdings here in the States?"

She nods fervently. "I'm on it." Her fingers fly over the keyboard as she works, her screen scrolling at a rapid pace.

"Aha! Here's something interesting. He purchased an abandoned property in Brooklyn a month ago. This article says construction isn't scheduled to start until next week.The only other buildings he owns on the East coast are fully operational hotels."

"It's a start," Royal says, "but I'm not convinced that Charles didn't take them to one of his functioning properties. He's not the type to take up residence in a derelict building."

"I disagree," I say. "Darnay's public persona is carefully curated. He wouldn't risk tarnishing his reputation by taking hostages to a location where they might be seen. He'd keep them far away from the prying eyes of the curious public. He'd take them to the abandoned property."

My dad and I make eye contact, and he squints, thinking through my reasoning. Finally, he nods. "You may be right."

Turning toward Haru, I shoot questions in rapid fire. "Can you give Royal the address of the abandoned building? Then find somewhere nearby where we can have a look without being seen? Avoid any CIA-associated buildings. We can't be sure what information Darnay has access to. We're on our own this time."

"Yes, ma'am!" Haru gives Royal the address, then opens a satellite view of the property on her laptop and starts scanning the surrounding area.

Clarity's stomach growls.

"Daniel?" Truly says, "I mean, Royal?"

My eyes go wide. Truly knows my dad's real name?

Lotus glances up, surprise showing on his features.

"Daniel? Is that your name?" Haru asks. "It suits you. You look like a Daniel."

"Shh," Clarity says. "Stop saying it out loud."

In the rearview mirror, I can see Royal schooling his

expression to hide a smile. "It's fine. I doubt we're being watched at the moment. But, Haru? Please refrain from using that name in the future."

"Sorry," Truly whispers. "It slipped out."

Royal gives her a sheepish smile, and Truly's cheeks blush a rosy pink. "Ahem. Should we find something to eat for lunch?"

"I could eat," I call from the back of the suburban.

Royal ignites the engine. "Then we'll pick something up. Quickly. And we'll eat in the car on our way to New York. Don't forget, we're under a time crunch."

How could I forget? Darnay has Gillian Harris, Starling, and Julep, and there's no telling what he's doing to them at this very moment.

Chapter 3

"We have to talk about Starling." Clarity's voice seeps into my consciousness.

I don't move, hoping the motion of the suburban will lull me back to sleep. The interior of the van smells like greasy french fries. A good smell.

A gentle finger pokes me in the arm.

With a groan, I open my eyes. "I just fell asleep," I mutter, lifting my eyes to meet my sister's where she's twisted in her seat, looking at me. Beyond her, Royal's eyes catch mine in the car's rearview mirror before flicking back to the road ahead.

"What is there to talk about?" Lotus spits. "He's a traitor. And when we catch him, he's going to get what's coming to him." His shoulders are corded with tension. I can't see his hands, but I'm guessing they're balled into fists.

Beside Clarity, Haru's cheeks go pale.

"You don't know that," I say, my voice level. "You can't do that."

"Watch me." Lotus's eyes burn into me, making me want to close them again to avoid this conversation.

"He apologized, so maybe he didn't mean to do it? Whatever happened?" Haru puts in over her shoulder.

"It's not good enough. I trusted him. We all did." Lotus ends with a grunt. "If I had been there…"

"You'd be dead. You saw what Darnay did to the body of Royal's co-worker. At this point, the man is beyond rational thought. He's driven by the desire for revenge."

"That's not comforting," Lotus grinds out.

"Didn't Julep used to work for Mr. Darnay?" Haru says in a tentative voice. "Maybe he liked her enough to take her with him?"

I don't respond. Darnay had liked Julep as an employee, and that goodwill was probably all that had kept her alive at Gillian Harris's house. There was no way to know how long it would last. Besides, Darnay wouldn't like her as an enemy combatant. She's a liability, as long as he keeps her alive. Gillian Harris may not have the skills to escape from the Cobalt Security guys, but Julep does. No matter how I look at it, Julep's time is running out, if it hasn't already expired.

Clarity's large eyes don't move from mine. Her fingers give my hand a squeeze. "Is there something you can tell us, anything that will help us understand?"

I bite my lip. "No, there's nothing I can say." It's the truth. There's nothing I can say to justify Starling's behavior to my teammates. No encouragement I can give them.

"How can you be so calm about this?" Lotus's voice is both angry and admonishing.

Frustration from the stress of the last several days builds in me, threatening to burst forth from every pore. "I don't have a choice." I hurl the words at him as if they were projectiles. "I can either trust Starling, or no one, ever again. There's no gray area. And I don't want to live like that. I can't."

Lotus rolls his eyes. "You're letting your feelings for him get in the way."

"And your feelings for Julep have no bearing on your actions right now?" I'm practically spitting with anger. We glare at each other, not speaking.

Clarity's hair ripples as she shakes her head, then turns to face front.

Haru, too, turns around, clutching Baron to her chest. The cat struggles to free itself, but Haru doesn't let go. Finally the giant furball stills, deigning to let the girl cuddle with him.

I refuse to meet Royal's gaze in the rearview mirror. I know exactly what he's thinking, and it looks like he was right.

Chapter 4

The alley where we're parked is bathed in darkness. At the entrance, the street light is out, broken by a carefully thrown rock. The sounds of the street are muffled by the line of brownstones to one side, and a sprawling brick building on the other side.

The air seeping in the cracks of our partially lowered car windows is crisp and cool, rippling over my skin and making the downy hairs on my arms stand on end. "You're up," I say, gripping the top of the seat in front of me.

Nodding, Clarity slips out of the suburban without making a sound. She creeps along the back of the building toward the fire escape. After glancing side to side, she leaps upward and catches the bottom rung of the metal ladder, using her weight to extend it toward the ground. Then, with careful steps, she scales it, mounting to the top. Taking a tool from her belt, she pops the lock on the window of the uppermost floor and disappears inside.

In a moment, the back door creaks open and she beckons us inside.

Royal steps out of the vehicle and scans the alley, checking for observant eyes one more time. But experience has taught me that no one will see us. No one is looking.

Lotus, Truly, and Haru slip out of the suburban and up the concrete steps into the house. Royal waits for me on the landing.

I'm clumsy crawling out of the suburban with my crutch. It slips out of my hands and clatters to the ground. The sound echoes off the brick, ricocheting toward the street at the end of the row. I freeze, my heart pounding in my chest. If someone heard the noise, will they come to investigate? My fingers inch toward my tranquilizer gun.

No lights flicker on in the windows facing the alley. No doors open. No curious eyes peer out to investigate the noise that cut through the night.

Royal shakes his head, waving me inside.

With one more glance toward the street, I swipe the crutch off the ground and hobble up the stairs into the building, the only sound the scuff of the rubber pad on the crutch as it grazes the ground.

I sigh in relief as Royal closes the door behind me, locking it securely and drawing the blind down over the small window.

"It was nice of Mr. and Mrs. Barclay to go out of town for the weekend, don't you think?" Haru asks, walking through the galley kitchen still clutching Baron in her hands. The cat wriggles free, jumps to the ground, and zips around the corner, between Truly and Clarity's legs.

"Not so smart to post about it on Facebook, though," I quip.

"I know. It's a good thing we're not robbers." Haru grins sheepishly.

Headlights from the cars along the street wash over the front room, then glide past.

"Damn. This is nice," Lotus says, running his hands over

the marble countertop. "Tell me why we live underground, again?"

"It was supposed to be more defensible…" Royal starts, but cuts himself off with a grunt.

I wave him off. "Never mind about that. We'll have to find a new home base anyway. The Ivory Tower is blown now that Cobalt Security knows where it's located. Let's sweep the place, then we'll get to work. Clarity, go through the house and make sure all window coverings are closed. Haru, keep a close eye on your cat. Actually, close all the doors to rooms we aren't using so he doesn't leave behind any more cat hair than is necessary." I sidle up to a shelf on the wall, studying the frames. "From the looks of it, the Barclays' cat is white, so if they find a ton of gray cat fur it'll raise a red flag."

Clarity draws the curtains tight over the large, bay window facing the street. They're not blackout curtains, so we can't risk turning on any lights inside the brownstone.

"What can I do?" Truly asks, still wearing her fluffy bathrobe.

I chew my lip and glance at the time on my watch. "First thing we need to do is get you some regular clothes. Get online and order a couple outfits. Have them rush shipped here. Don't use your real name, email address, anything."

"All right." She walks around to the front of the tweedy green couch and sits, pulling out her phone.

I follow her, easing myself down and propping my injured leg on the antique wood coffee table. "Lotus. Order us some dinner. I'm starved." The tacos we got from a drive-through place wore off hours ago.

"Yes, ma'am." He plops down in a slouchy camel-colored chair, pulls out his phone, and immediately opens his favorite restaurant app.

One by one, all of my teammates return to the living room, having completed the assignments I gave them. When we're all seated on the cozy furniture, piping hot pizza in our hands, we begin. I take a big bite of the savory pepperoni pie, enjoying the taste of melted cheese on my tongue.

Haru kneels at the coffee table, her fingers whizzing over her laptop screen. She spins it so I can see. "Here are the photos I found of the property Mr. Darnay purchased. According to the articles I found, construction hasn't started yet, so it's empty. The electricity isn't on, as far as I can tell, and neither are the other utilities."

I narrow my eyes, considering this.

"If I know Charles," Royal speaks, "he'll have security over every inch of the place. He wouldn't have chosen it if it weren't easily fortified. He'll have cameras and motion sensors, not to mention an untold number of Cobalt Security personnel at his disposal."

Haru shoves the sleeves of her dandelion yellow hoodie up to her elbows and flicks through the building's listing photos again, keeping back so everyone can see the images.

I study each one, looking for access points. Not the front door; that would be too obvious. Not the back door either. The underground parking garage looks like it was recently the home of a group of squatters, and wading through all of that debris would be tricky.

"The roof. That's our entry point."

Royal meets my gaze. "I agree. It'll give us the high ground, at least."

Lotus nods, studying the images of the building's roofline. "Shouldn't be too hard to get in from there." He's right; there's a large skylight right in the center of the building's roof. A minute with my glass cutter is all it'll take to get inside, assuming the glass isn't pressure or heat sensitive.

"When are we going in?" I ask, still reclined on the couch.

A muscle in Royal's jaw clenches. "You aren't going anywhere. You are staying behind with Haru and Truly."

"Like hell I am." I shove to my feet, wincing at the pain in my injured leg. My hand grips my crutch as I straighten to my full height. "I'm going."

"You're not." Royal's voice is flat, unmoving.

"You can't stop me."

"I'll chain you to this table if I have to. I'd use handcuffs, but—"

"I'll get out of them."

"You're injured. You're in no condition to stage an assault on a building with who knows what sorts of security measures. You'd be a liability to us. You know that."

Clarity reaches out with a slender hand and grabs my free hand. "He's right, sis. You'll be the most help here, providing watchful eyes." She squeezes my fingers before letting go.

My gaze drops to where my knuckles are white on my crutch. The words sting, but they're true. I'm not in top condition, and if there's a skirmish in Darnay's building, and I'll be shocked if there isn't, my dad will need only people in top shape. People who are operating at peak physical condition. People like Lotus and Clarity. As much as I resist, this is one of those times when I have to rely on my teammates instead of doing everything myself. I force my gaze up to meet my dad's eyes. "Fine. I'll stay here. For now."

"Good." He stands to stretch.

Truly's eyes flicker to him and her cheeks flush.

Clarity lifts her eyebrows and smirks at me.

"Yeah, yeah," I mouth to her.

She stands and arches backward, arms flung wide. "I'm

exhausted," she breathes.

"Me too," Lotus adds. "Is it nap time yet?"

"That sounds amazing," Clarity says.

Royal's eyes scan each of us. "Everyone get a couple of hours of sleep. We go in at 04:00."

"Um, Royal?" Haru pipes up, her fingers pressing her laptop closed.

"Yes?"

"What if it's a trap?"

"Oh, it's definitely a trap."

Her face goes tight. "But we don't have a choice, do we?"

"No, Haru, we don't."

Resolve pools in my belly. If we want to rescue Gillian Harris, and find Starling, he's right. We have no choice at all.

Chapter 5

Royal said I had to stay behind. He didn't specify where,
exactly. I can't help the smile that parts my lips as I scale the
fire escape, using mostly my arms and my one good leg to pull
my body up the rungs of cold metal. An icy wind whips over
me, pressing the lapels of my trench coat tighter to my neck.

Down at ground level, something scurries behind the
garbage bin, making the crumpled up old newspapers rustle.
I'm wishing I'd brought Baron with me. With his great size,
surely he's a good mouser. Or ratter, as the case may be.

I push the grimace off my face and focus on the ladder.

Up above, the slate gray sky is hazy with reflected light.
Even this early, it's not as dark as one might expect.

My fingers grip another rung and I pull myself up ever
higher toward the roof.

Haru is already in position up there, prepared to back our
team with the weaponized drone we brought with us. Won't
she be surprised to see me.

I'm only a couple of rungs away from the top when I lose
grip on my crutch. It clangs loudly against the ladder. The
vibrations in the metal course through my body. I go still,
waiting for the movement to subside before I climb up the rest

of the way.

Across the street, Royal, Lotus, and Clarity are scaling another, almost identical fire escape. Hopefully they're quieter than me. I let out a low curse of frustration. This stupid crutch is only slowing me down. I can't wait to be rid of it, but Dr. Faraday was vague about how long I'd need it.

The sound of movement on the roof catches my attention, making me crane my neck to get a look.

A pair of dark eyes peers down over the side of the building, face pale, hands shaking as unpracticed fingers grip a tranquilizer gun. It's pointed more or less straight at my head.

My pulse increases. She's not going to shoot me, is she?

Haru's sigh is ragged as she spots me. "It's you!" she whisper-yells. "You scared me. What are you doing here? Royal told you to—"

"He told me I couldn't go in with them. He didn't say anything about having to stay in the brownstone. In fact, he stipulated that I had to stay with you, so here I am."

"Shh!" Haru cocks her head, thinking through our conversation. She must realize that, technically, I'm right, because she holsters her gun and extends her hand. "Then let's get you up on the roof."

I take her outstretched arm. "Excellent."

"Remind me to take you for shooting practice once we're back in D.C." I say after we're both firmly on the flat, gravelly roof.

She flushes with embarrassment.

"Hey, don't worry about it. I used to be just like you. All you need is practice." Eyeing the way she's holding the tranquilizer gun pointed down at her own food, I add, "A lot of practice."

Her ponytail swishes in the wind. "Thanks." She holsters

the gun awkwardly.

"So, what have we got?"

"I'm all set up over there."

I follow her pointed finger to a sheltered spot beside a large utility housing. Her laptop sits in the dark beside it, giving her a good view of the hotel next door. "I've got the cameras from the drone streaming on my desktop," she whispers, moving across the rough surface to sink down in her spot. "I don't have any extra earbuds. Sorry."

For the first time, I'm thankful for the whine of the wind. Without it, someone stationed near the roof of the hotel would hear the low buzz of the drone easily and know something was coming. Looking up at the dark sky, I can't spot it anywhere.

I shrug and sink down beside her, propping my crutch against the side of the shed. "No worries. I'm just here to watch."

Haru lets out a disbelieving sniff, but doesn't elaborate. Instead, she pulls her hood up around her head and pulls the strings to tighten it around her face.

"So, where is everyone?"

"They're in position on the roof. They'll be ready to go in one minute."

"So what you're saying is I have perfect timing."

Haru goes still, listening to one of my teammates on her earbud. "Yes? Okay. I'll tell her." She turns to me. "Royal says that if you so much as look at the hotel too hard, he'll shoot you himself."

I snort. "Okay. Sure."

She relays my response, then pauses to listen. "We're ready when you are." She scans the footage from the drone. "The coast is clear. Go ahead."

In the footage, which is tinted green on the night-vision

setting, I can see Clarity using my lazer cutter to remove a pane of glass from the large skylight on the roof of the building across the street. Lotus lifts the pane out of its hole and prepares a climbing rope to belay Clarity down into the building.

My teammates move in slow, precise movements, but it doesn't take them long to disappear inside the massive, darkened edifice.

I scan the rooftop, but there's no sign of movement around us.

There's an ache in my chest, a longing to be with them, in the thick of the mission. "Is this what it feels like, always being on the outside? Never on the front lines?"

Haru's forehead creases in confusion. "I guess so. I'm thankful to be here. I'd never want to be in there, responsible for other people. Shooting and being shot at." She gives an exaggerated shiver.

"It's such a rush," I say, "knowing what I'm capable of, and helping other people."

Haru merely "Hmms," in response, her eyes focused on the drone footage.

Not knowing how to respond to that, I purse my lips together.

Minutes go by in silence. It's eerie, watching my teammates as the drone hovers behind them, winding through the hotel. They move in stealth silence, scanning each room they come to in perfect formation. For an almost-retired guy, Royal is as great an operative as ever.

Time stretches out as they search the building, encountering neither friend nor foe.

I chew on the inside of my lip. If this mission is going to be so boring, maybe they don't need me after all.

But my stomach won't unclench. Something doesn't feel right. Either Darnay isn't here, or it's a trap my team has just walked right into.

My team maneuvers around a corner into what looks like a large conference room. Graffiti lines the walls, and there's trash littered all over the floor. In the center, there are two figures tied to what looks like wooden chairs. Gillian Harris and Julep.

"They've found them!" Haru says, clapping silently.

In the footage, Clarity moves toward them and begins to assess their condition.

"COO Harris and Julep are both alive," Haru says.

My instincts hum as I scan the room for any sign of Darnay or his men.

Maybe I was wrong. Maybe it will be this easy. I pump my fist. "Yes! And Starling?"

She gives a little head shake. "Royal says there's no sign of him."

He's not with them. Well, crap.

"But where are all of the Cobalt guys? Where is all of the security Royal said Darnay would have?" I mutter aloud.

Haru shrugs. "Maybe he didn't have time to put anything in place?"

I shake my head. "No, something's wrong here. This is too easy. It's either the wrong place, or..." I'm cut off as a scream of warning echoes through Haru's comms.

She freezes. "Someone's there."

Something dark swings toward the drone's camera, destroying it with a direct hit. The feed cuts out, and our screen goes black.

Chapter 6

Haru gasps in surprise and pushes at the control panel on her screen. "It's not responding," she exclaims, jabbing harder.

Muted gunshots filter into the air from the hotel.

My companion hunkers down lower on the wall, gripping her laptop with determined fingers.

"Hey, you're safe here," I say, drawing my weapon. "Don't worry."

Haru's head bobs in acknowledgement of my words, but she doesn't loosen her grip on her computer.

I lift my eyes toward the hotel opposite, and that's when I see it. There's movement on the roof. Four figures have shimmied up the fire escape and are inching toward the skylight where my teammates entered the building.

Haru and I were too busy watching the drone footage to notice.

I curse under my breath. Some lookout I turned out to be.

From their outlines, I can tell the men on the roof opposite have some serious weaponry this time.

"Haru, warn them. Four incoming from the roof." I push forward onto all fours, ignoring the pain in my thigh.

Haru's whispering hurriedly, updating my teammates on

the guys headed straight for them. From the sounds of gunshots in the hotel, they're already taking fire. My skin crawls. What if they're pinned down? What if they're injured, or worse?

I shove the thought down. There's no use thinking about that right now.

My eyes are glued to the four men as they move toward the door leading inside, taking careful steps in case one of my teammates is lying in wait.

But none of them are.

It's up to me now.

I crawl over the gravel rooftop as tiny bits of rock gouge into my hands and knees. I ignore the sharp, needling pains in my skin. The edge of the roof looms, and I duck down behind the three-foot tall brick sill. Hopefully it'll provide the cover I need.

Far too quickly the Cobalt guys have the door open and are gesturing to each other to advance inside.

With painstakingly slow movements, I raise the barrel of my gun over the rough edge of the brick, aim, and fire.

The bullet connects with the side of one man's head, right through the ear. He goes down immediately. Dead.

His three teammates swivel toward me, scrambling for cover inside the doorway. Hopefully I'll be able to keep them busy for a few minutes, buy my teammates some time.

Gunshots ring out and bullets fly over my head.

My eyes shoot to where Haru is huddled on her stomach on the ground, still trying to recall the drone using the keys on her laptop. Her face is pained, but her fingers are steady. She's turning out to be pretty handy in a pinch.

There's a break in the shooting, so I steal a glance over the sill. Aim. Fire. Duck.

I'm not positive, but I think I hit another one of them. Not in a vital spot, unfortunately, but he's definitely wounded. Hopefully my teammates are able to get Gillian Harris and Julep out of there.

More shots whizz over my head, and others pummel the brick of the sill. I inch away from the point of impact rather than counting on the brick to protect me. Peeking over the side, I squeeze off another couple of shots. Another Cobalt guy goes down.

I duck, pressing my body flat against the surface of the roof, ignoring the sensation of the gravel poking into my cheek.

The air reeks of gunpowder. I confess it's such a familiar smell, it doesn't bother me like it probably should.

Sirens cut through the air, their wails coming closer. Reinforcements are on their way.

In an instant, the gunshots go silent, on the hotel's roof, and inside the building. What's going on over there?

But I don't dare look. We're in a deadly game of whack-a-mole, and I do not want to be the mole.

Seconds tick by in silence. My heart pounds, slamming against my ribcage. Gingerly, I turn my face toward Haru, who is focused on her laptop screen.

"Anything?" I ask, hoping she's the only one who can hear me.

She merely shakes her head, not taking her eyes off the screen.

I bite my lip. What's going on in there?

The scream of sirens announces the arrival of the police on the street below.

A relieved sigh escapes me. Maybe they'll catch Darnay, and this will all be over.

I push up onto my hands and knees and peek over the side

of the building. Below us, red and blue lights bathe the brick facades in harsh flashes. The police take up positions, preparing to enter the building, weapons at the ready.

I scan the abandoned hotel, looking for signs of movement, but with all of the lights off inside it's impossible to see anything.

Haru scrabbles up beside me, clutching her laptop to her chest. "That was close."

"How is everyone? We all okay?"

Haru goes quiet.

"What? Who is it?"

"COO Harris, she was shot. They don't know if she's going to make it."

My heart falls. If she dies, there will be another body to lay at Darnay's feet. My teeth clench. We have to stop him. I can't imagine the pain he has experienced as he wondered what really happened to his wife for the past twenty years, but no amount of killing will make up for it.

"Look!" Haru whispers, pointing to the ground floor of the hotel.

The police march two men and two women out of the building in handcuffs. My teammates.

Behind them, two more support an injured woman between them. They carry her straight to the waiting ambulance and lay her on a stretcher.

No one else exits the building.

"That's it? They didn't catch Darnay? Or even any Cobalt guys?"

Haru shakes her head. "He got away. They all got away."

I frown. "What sort of game is he playing?"

The EMTs hover over Gillian Harris, trying to staunch the bleeding from a wound in her chest. It doesn't look like she's going to make it.

Chapter 7

The ambulance workers are still trying to stabilize Gillian Harris when Haru and I totter up the sidewalk toward the hotel. A crowd has gathered in the early morning. Runners stand alongside homeless people, gaping at the police cars still lining the sidewalk. The sirens have been silenced, but the red and blue lights still glow over the crowd.

"Let us through!" Haru says, trying her best to push people aside so the two of us can get to the front of the group.

Several people glare at her, but they stop when they see me using a crutch. I play it up, limping as I walk, so they'll get out of my way. Since I'm injured, I might as well use it to my advantage.

It works. The crowd parts and I press against the police tape, scanning the clump of officers. It only takes a second for me to find them: Royal, Clarity, and Lotus, huddled near the back of a second ambulance. Julep sits on the tailgate as an EMT looks her over. Royal is talking in a low voice to one of the officers, probably getting them up to speed on Darnay's road trip of terror.

With a smooth sweep of my hand, I'm under the yellow tape and pelting across the road toward them.

"Stop!" one of the police officers yells at me, but I ignore him. I have to get to my family, see that they're safe.

A hand grips my shoulder, pulling me back. "I said stop. You aren't allowed here."

I turn a withering glare onto the police officer holding my arm. He's average height with ruddy skin and a mustache. He doesn't flinch under my look.

"Let go of me. Now."

His fingers press into my skin. "You're not allowed here. You have to get back behind the tape."

"That's my family," I grind out. "You have to let me see them." My fingers tighten on my crutch. If push comes to shove, it would make a handy weapon.

"Can you provide some identification?"

"She's okay. It's my daughter." Royal jogs over to us and puts an arm around me. "This is my daughter."

Haru creeps up on Royal's other side, hugging close to him.

"And my other daughter." My dad slips his free arm around her shoulders.

The officer's eyes widen, flicking from us to Clarity and back. "You... You have three daughters. And a son? And they're not all... they're..."

"Adopted. Yes."

The officer's mouth opens to respond, but Royal pivots us away from him. "Thanks for the assist, earlier," he whispers to me as he ushers us up onto the sidewalk next to Lotus and Clarity. "Haru filled me while she was waiting for you to climb down that fire escape. Nice work."

My smile is tight. "You're welcome. Happy to help."

"Hey," Lotus says, lifting his chin in greeting. "Couldn't stay away, could ya?"

A smile crosses my face. I don't even mind the teasing. I'm just glad he's talking to me again. "Nope."

"Thankfully," Clarity puts in, coming to give me a hug. "It was pretty close in there. We're lucky we got out."

"About that, what happened?" I push back from my sister to meet her eyes. "The last thing I saw was the drone being rammed."

Clarity nods. "Darnay had some of his security guys waiting behind a false wall. They took out the drone before we could stop them. They almost had us surrounded, but Haru managed to get the drone to fire on them from the floor. It gave us the opportunity we needed to get past them, out of that room."

"Wow. So… Did you see…?"

"Starling? No." But her eyes skitter away from mine. There's something she's not telling me.

"What? What is it?"

Clarity swings her eyes back to mine. "You're not going to like it."

"Just tell me."

She looks toward where Julep is sitting, swatting the EMT away. Lotus hovers near her, hands in his pockets. "Julep told us that Starling was the one who tied them up. He gagged them and everything."

My heart drops. "He did?"

"Yes. And then he left them there."

I'm shaking my head involuntarily. I will it to stop. "No. He wouldn't. His relationship with his dad is crap. He's on our side."

"It doesn't look that way. I'm sorry." She whispers the last word, and reaches out to hug me again.

I'm like stone under my sister's touch. Her words swirl in

my head. Starling tied them up. He left them there. He was working with Darnay. Other thoughts emerge, warring with the first. He's part of our team. He said he'd always wanted to fit in somewhere, have a family. He said he liked me. He wanted to take me on a real date, like two normal teenagers.

I clench my teeth. He wasn't lying. He couldn't have been. I would have been able to tell. Wouldn't I?

But the look on Clarity's face ignites a flicker of doubt in me. Is it possible Starling *was* lying? That he had me fooled, just like Darnay did in London? I shake it off. No, it's not possible. Fool me once? Shame on you. But fool me twice and, well, I should hang up my spying gear right now.

The EMTs close the back door to the ambulance and pull away, their siren ear-splittingly loud. It's time to get Harris more help.

Royal comes over to us, his expression grim.

"Dad? What is it?" Clarity asks, hovering closer to him.

He motions for us to move farther away from the crowd until we're huddled against the hotel. Police still move in and out of the building. To one side, a coroner's van has been parked at the curb. How many of Darnay's men have fallen? I look around at my own family. Once again, we were lucky. Apart from some scrapes and bruises, every one of them walked out of that building unassisted.

"Before she was taken to the hospital, COO Harris gave me some information that may help us. She overheard Starling telling one of the other men that he was meeting his father at the airport."

"They're fleeing the country," I say. "It's what I would do if I had the CIA after me."

Royal cocks his head. "Not exactly."

"Then what are they doing? Everyone they're after is right

here." I wave a hand across the circle we've formed on the sidewalk. Above us, the first streaks of light from the dawning sun fan out across the sky, sending out ribbons of fuschia pink across the gray clouds.

"Starling said that he and his father were heading to Georgia."

They're heading to Georgia? Why does that sound familiar?

Julep goes still. "Georgia? Was she sure?"

Royal nods. "Yes. She said she heard it clearly."

Julep's hand snakes out and snatches Lotus's arm, her fingers gripping tightly.

Lotus winces, but doesn't pull away.

When Julep meets Royal's gaze, there are angry sparks shooting from her eyes. "My grandmother lives in Georgia."

Chapter 8

I munch absently on the everything bagel in my hand. We stopped for them on our way out of New York, before we started the drive back to D.C.

My sister sits in the seat beside me, whispering to Uncle Nestore on her phone. She told him the bare minimum of information: that she would be out of touch for a few days because we were going on a trip. When he asked her where we were going, she merely told him we were going to visit relatives. She says goodbye in Italian, and then hangs up her phone and tucks it between her legs.

In the seat in front of us, Lotus is sitting next to Julep. She's clinging to his hand for all she's worth, her lips moving in what look like whispered prayers. Her initial anger has dissolved into worry.

Lotus leans over and whispers something to her, but whatever he says, it does nothing to relieve the tension in her muscles. Even her hair seems rigid with anxiety about the state of her defenseless, super old grandma.

I can't stop thinking about what she said in front of the hotel, about Starling tying up Julep and Gillian Harris and leaving them in the hotel. It sounds like he's working with his dad, but I simply can't accept that. If he is, it brings up so many questions. I think back over everything he said to me, sifting through it. His confessions about his strained relationship with his father, his aunt who raised him, his contentment at finding a team who accepted him and made him feel like an integral part. The sensation of his lips on mine rises to the forefront, making my pulse race. I can't think about that now. I have to get some answers. "Julep?"

She swivels in her seat to look at me, her lips parted.

"What happened once you and Starling arrived at Gillian Harris's house?" I haven't heard the story yet, and I have to know.

Julep's head bobs. "We were moving along the side of the house, and the side gate was open."

This whole scenario sounds familiar. My mind flashes back to another abandoned home. A dumpy motel. A dingy room filled with the overwhelming stench of a rotting corpse.

Clarity puts a hand on my leg.

I swallow, forcing the disturbing images away. "Go ahead."

Julep fidgets with the hem of her shirt. "I thought I saw something moving in the backyard, in the treeline, so I told Starling. I readied my weapon, just in case I needed it. I wasn't in the fight at the Tower, but I heard enough of it to know that the Cobalt Security forces are not to be underestimated. I was about to tell Starling to do the same when he... hit me. Knocked me out cold."

My mouth drops open in shock and my insides twist. "Then what happened?"

"He must have carried me to their vehicle, because I woke up in the back of a van, handcuffed and gagged. Gillian Harris was on the floor next to me. I would have tried to escape, somehow, but one of their guys had a gun trained on me the entire time. And Starling, he sat in the front passenger seat, not even bothering to glance back at me. He didn't say a word the entire drive." Fire ignites behind her eyes. "If I get my hands on him—"

"You'll arrest him and we'll take him in, like we're supposed to do." My words are firm, brooking no argument.

"Not if I get to him first," Lotus spits, eyes narrowed.

"You will not harm him, unless absolutely necessary," Royal says from the driver seat. "We do everything by the rules. Anyone who disobeys me will be removed from the field immediately."

Lotus grits his teeth, glaring at the back of Royal's seat.

"And when you got to the hotel, he tied both of you up, gagged you, and left?"

She nods. "Yes. I was surprised at how cold he acted toward me. I was the one who met him in England and brought him to the U.S. We spent weeks together training before he moved into the Tower." Her eyes fall. "It was like he didn't know me at all. We weren't even friends."

Doubts swirl through me as I look away, out the window at the morning sky. I don't know what to say, so I don't say anything at all.

The small, private airport where Royal keeps his plane is fairly busy this morning. Grounds personnel dot the tarmac, orchestrating the movements of small planes in the line to take off using the smooth, solitary runway. Others place traffic cones or pull carts of equipment to and from the two small hangars that run along the fence.

Royal pulls the suburban to a stop at the security gate,

shows the guard some identification, and thanks him when the red and white striped security arm is raised. He pulls the vehicle into the airport and drives slowly toward the last hangar. "It's a good thing that backstabbing jerk doesn't know where you keep your plane," Lotus says, his eyes scanning the yard.

"Indeed."

Julep stiffens, then leans toward the window, peering out.

"What is it?" I ask, looking out my window in the same direction.

She shakes her head. "I thought I saw... but it can't be. I must be getting paranoid."

"Okay..." I draw out the word, not sure what to make of this. I scan the yard, but don't see anything suspicious. There's a man carrying shipping boxes from inside one of the hangars to a waiting car outside it, but he's the only one who bothers with glancing us before going back to work. He hardly looks threatening.

Royal parks the car and slides out. In a move that both surprises and pleases me, he walks around the car and opens Truly's door, taking her hand to help her out of the vehicle. It's both super cute and super weird, watching him attend to her like this.

I clamber out of the car after my sister, who watches to make sure I don't fall on my face. But I swing my crutch to the ground and brace myself. I'm getting the hang of it.

"I wish you were somewhere safe," Royal whispers to Truly, "but I can't be sure if any of the CIA safe houses are secure. I hope you understand."

Truly gives him a shy smile. "I do. Thank you."

Royal straightens and glances at the rest of us, who are hovering nearby, watching the two of them. "Ahem. Let's go. Wheels up as soon as I do the pre-flight checks."

We respond with a chorus of, "Yes, sirs," and make our way toward the hangar.

"I sure wish I had a change of clothes," Clarity says, trying to smooth the wrinkles in her blouse. The creamy fabric is crinkled and smudged with dust, and the rest of us don't look much better. Haru's hoodie is streaked with what looks like black tar, probably from the rooftop bac in New York. And Lotus's red shorts are torn near the knee. Actually, it might be a bullet hole.

Haru sighs, carting Baron over one shoulder. The cat glares at me, yellow eyes snapping in indignation.

"Hey, it's not my fault you're being dragged all over creation," I say with a forced laugh. "Blame Charles Darnay."

The cat hisses this time, teeth bared.

My steps hitch, letting Haru get further away. "That cat doesn't like me," I whisper to my sister.

"To be fair, the cat doesn't like anyone but Haru," Clarity whispers back, watching the beast.

To the left, a plane advances along the runway, picking up speed.

I stop to watch as the craft's front wheels lift. It's back wheels leap off the ground, and the plane rises into the sky, the sound of its engines rumbling over the airport.

I don't even see the guy aiming his gun at me until his first bullet cracks through the air, whizzing a mere hairsbreadth away from my arm.

Cries go up from airport crewmen around us as they scramble for cover under planes and behind the hangars themselves. One man ducks behind a luggage cart.

"Loveday!"

I whirl around, drawing my weapon and firing at the man crouched just inside the opposite hangar. He ducks out of sight.

"Run!" Royal calls, pulling Truly into the open door of the building.

Lotus, Julep, and Haru careen through the door, ducking as more shots are fired.

Clarity looks at me, face stricken.

"Come on!" I yell, striding forward as quickly as I can on a bum leg.

A hand snakes out and grabs my free arm, yanking me around.

I react by instinct, whipping my crutch off the ground and bringing it slamming down into the man's neck where it meets the shoulder.

He cries out in pain, dropping his hand off my arm.

Another swing of my crutch ends with a crunch as the man's knee buckles.

He sprawls on the ground, holding his knee in both hands and groaning in pain.

Serves him right, putting hands on me like that.

Clarity's arm snakes around my waist, and she hoists me up off the ground, barreling toward the open hangar door with me pressed to her side.

I keep hold of the crutch with my other hand, my body bouncing against my sister's.

Several more gunshots rend the air, making Clarity's eyes widen in terror and sweat break out on her temples. She grits her teeth, clutching at me even as my weight slows her down.

"Put me down!" I growl. I struggle to twist around so I can see our attackers, but Clarity's holding me so tight it's all I can do just to hold on.

More shots careen past us, and Clarity attempts to zig zag like a wild hare.

From the hangar, Royal and Julep crack off a couple of

shots, providing us with cover.

I cling to Clarity as she moves, frankly surprised neither of us has been hit. The Cobalt guys are losing their touch. There's no other explanation. Unless they're shooting wide on purpose.

A bullet flies past my head, missing by a millimeter. So much for their shots being purposely off target.

We reach the hangar. My sister practically leaps inside, flinging me into the building.

Royal, Lotus, and Julep close around us, guarding the door with their weapons raised.

More gunshots rattle the corrugated metal walls.

"Get down!" I yell, pulling Haru onto the ground beside me. On her other side, Truly hunkers against the concrete, her face white with strain.

Royal and Lotus fire at our aggressors, then duck inside the building. "Two down, one to go," Lotus says.

Royal checks his clip. Finding it empty, he pockets it and inserts a new one.

"Where?" Julep asks, checking her own gun.

"Three o'clock."

Julep takes a deep breath, waits for a break in the fire, and takes a shot.

It's silent, inside and outside the hangar.

Nobody moves.

The scent of gunpowder permeates the air. That smell seems to follow us wherever we go.

The absence of the rumble of planes and the calls of airport workers on the ground is eerie and unnerving.

"Third suspect is down," Julep says, sagging against the wall.

"Who were those guys?" Lotus asks, holstering his weapon. "More Cobalt guys?"

I shake my head. "I don't think so."

Julep bites her lip, glancing between Royal and Clarity.

My sister sits up straighter, eyes wide. "What? Why are you looking at me?"

Julep takes a step toward us. "I know them. I've seen them before."

"Where?" I ask, righting my crutch and pulling to a stand. "Did they work for Darnay? In London?"

She shakes her head. Her eyes fasten on Clarity. "In Boston. When I was undercover? With the Sicilian mafia?"

My blood runs cold. If those men are from the Sicilian mafia, there's only one way they could have found us. I lurch toward my sister, hand outstretched. "Clarity, where's your phone?"

"My phone? Why?" She withdraws, trembling.

Before she can stop me, I snatch the phone out of her pocket, throw it to the ground, and slam the end of my crutch down on the device with a loud crack. The glass screen shatters as it splinters apart.

"Why did you do that?" my sister complains, kneeling to poke at the destroyed phone. I had hundreds of photos saved on my phone."

"Think it through," I say in my best soothing voice. She may not have put it together yet, but I already know. If the men who attacked us are from the Sicilian mob, there's only one possible reason they're here. Clarity's dear uncle Nestore used her cell phone to track us, and sent his men to kill us. Probably in retaliation for imprisoning Beppe Arnoni. So much for him being a decent human being.

Clarity's eyebrows knit together and her mouth forms a shocked O. She's figured it out. And then she bursts into tears.

Chapter 9

Royal's expression is grim as he climbs down from the small aircraft. His plane is not flying anywhere today. "I don't know what they did to it, exactly, but it's enough to keep us from flying to Georgia."

"Then we find another plane." Julep's voice is urgent as she keeps watch on the airport via the hangar door, back rigid and gun poised.

Beside her, Lotus nods.

It was yet another mess for Royal to explain to the local law enforcement officers who showed up after our gunfight, but he managed. Once they were convinced of our alignment with the CIA, they set to work clearing the bodies from the scene. I swallow, looking out the window at the small airport, where all that remains of the bodies of the Sicilians is the dark red blood on the asphalt.

After the officers left, Royal climbed into his plane to prepare for takeoff, but it looks like the Sicilians made sure we wouldn't be able to make a quick getaway by plane. At least, not with this one.

I chew my lip. Should I offer to make a call?

Royal walks over to Truly and puts an arm around her.

"I'm sorry about all this."

"Is it always like this?" She whispers.

"No. There aren't usually so many bullets involved."

At my back, Clarity mutters, "No kidding."

Truly nods, her shoulders relaxing. She exhales deeply and leans into his side.

My dad goes still with his head tilted down toward Truly and his eyes fastened on her face. "Once we've captured Charles, I'm thinking of making a change."

My eyebrows fly upward. Is he suggesting what I think he is?

As if reading my mind, Royal looks over at me.

I straighten up, leaning as little weight on my crutch as I can muster. If I'm right, I need to look as capable and physically fit as I possibly can, given the walking apparatus and the bandage around my thigh.

"Loveday, everyone, gather around." He gestures for all of us to approach, and waits while we oblige.

"I'm staying on lookout," Julep says, not moving from the doorway, "so speak up."

Royal nods. His eyes travel over each of us, a serious look etched into his features.

Clarity scoots in behind me, draping her arms over my shoulders and resting her chin on the top of my head. "It's nice that you're so short. You make a good headrest."

"Yeah, yeah," I say even though I can't help but smile.

Lotus sidles up beside Haru and gives her a bump with his hip. She grins in return, her cheeks rosy in the chilly air.

"I was going to wait until we were finished with this job," Royal begins, "but you might as well know. Once we bring Charles Darnay and Starling into custody—"

"And the rest of the Cobalt Security guys," Lotus adds.

"Yes, them too. Once we've completed this job, I'm retiring."

"But you're already retired," I blurt.

My dad's eyes level on me. "I am semi-retired, but I want to stop completely. That means I won't be setting up jobs for you, anymore. And I'll find a new place to live, above ground."

My jaw hardens. His announcement has caught me completely off guard. First he's dating Truly, and now he wants to quit CIA work completely? "What about our team? We'll have to find a new base of operations, and establish a link with whoever takes over COO Harris's job." Yet another loss, even though I didn't know the woman well. We'd gotten word that she'd been declared DOA at the hospital.

Royal withdraws his arm from Truly's waist and walks toward me, his steps determined. Our eyes lock as he lifts his hands to my shoulders.

I wait, my breaths coming shallow. My eyes drop to the floor. What is he going to say? That we're done? That my career in espionage is over? First Clarity wants out, and now my dad? Not to mention Starling's apparent alliance with Darnay. I grit my teeth. My team is starting to look more like Swiss cheese than a cohesive unit.

"Loveday."

I force myself to meet my dad's eyes.

"I've been watching you closely over the past several months. I've never seen such composure, such skill in one so young. You are ready to lead this team. I have no doubt that you can become one of the best assets the CIA has ever had, if that's what you wish to do. Is that what you want?"

Again he surprises me, but this time in a good way. My heart leaps in my chest at my dad's praise. I nod my head, my tongue tripping over any thanks I try to muster.

His fingers press into my shoulders. "Then you're in charge now. You've made me proud." Then he lets go, turning to the rest of the team. "Does anyone have an idea for how to transport us to Georgia?"

"We could drive," Lotus says, scratching at the back of his neck with one hand. "I bet I could get us there in good time."

"That would take hours," Julep calls from the door. "We need a plane."

I tap the foot of my crutch on the ground. Tap. Tap. "I may know a guy."

Royal's eyes meet mine. And he smiles.

Chapter 10

The screech of a plane engine rips through the atmosphere, drawing my attention upward to the small private aircraft that's roaring along the runway, its landing gear extending toward the earth like a swan gliding to a landing on the water of a still, quiet lake. It taxis over the asphalt, turning toward where I'm standing in the door of the hangar.

Julep pushes off the door frame, uncrossing her arms and letting out a loud sigh. "Finally." She takes her phone out of her pocket, glances at the screen, then stows it again.

"She still hasn't called you back?"

She merely shakes her head.

"Are you sure there's no chance she's simply not hearing the phone ring?"

Julep shoots a worried look my way. "She keeps the ringer up louder than a foghorn. There's no way she'd miss it. I just hope she's all right."

Extending my hand, I pat her arm. "We're going to get there in time. Your grandma is going to be just fine."

Julep's heavy eyes lift to mine, and she gives a slight nod.

I probably shouldn't be making those sorts of promises, since it appears that Darnay has gone down to Georgia expressly to harass Julep's grandmother and smoke us out, but there's nothing else I can do in the meantime. Platitudes are all I have. Platitudes and Pete.

The plane slows as it reaches the hangar, coming to a stop mere feet away from where we're standing.

Pete waves to me from the cockpit, his graying hair sticking out from behind the headphones he's wearing.

I wave back, noticing that the co-pilot's seat is vacant. Apparently Adnan wasn't available on such short notice. Shrugging, I turn toward where the rest of my team is loitering inside the corrugated metal structure.

Royal and Truly are sitting in the cockpit of his plane. The way she's smiling makes it clear she's enjoying his explanation of how he pilots the small aircraft.

Haru is cuddling with Baron, who looks pretty relaxed stretched out over the girl's legs. The cat is licking her fingers, eating any remnants of the tuna salad she fed him from one of the terminal vending machines.

Clarity is sprawled out on the ground, reading a book with arms holding it straight up in the air. Her brunette hair makes a halo around her head. I study her, wondering how she's doing with the knowledge that she put a bullet through a man's brain less than twelve hours ago. She must feel the weight of my eyes on her, because she glances my way and gives me a faint smile before returning to her book. It's a tiny gesture, but it's reassuring. Somehow, I think she's going to be okay.

Lotus hovers a few feet behind Julep, hands in his pockets. He straightens at my look and moves toward me.

"Looks like you're co-piloting," I toss out, gesturing toward the cockpit of the newly arrived plane.

He pumps his fist and walks past me out of the hangar, snagging the rolling stairs and pushing them toward the door of the aircraft, where Pete's waiting. "I thought you were in a hurry," he calls. "Where is everyone?"

"We are," I yell back. "Wheels up in ten minutes!"

"Roger that." He disappears within the plane.

Lotus climbs up the stairs, taking two at a time, and follows Pete inside.

Julep bustles across the asphalt to the plane and scales the stairs in a hurry. At the top, she takes her phone out of her pocket and puts it to her ear. Hopefully her grandma will answer this time. But from Julep's frustrated hiss and the way she shoves the phone in the pocket whence it came, I'm guessing not.

I'm trying not to worry about the old woman, telling myself that if Starling is with Darnay, he'll prevent the older man from harming her. It's a small comfort, considering the question mark over Starling's status, but I have to be optimistic. If I start letting worry get to me, it'll affect my entire team. My team. I can't help the small smile that rises at this. All of my hard work is starting to pay off. My dad's words of praise echo through me, making me stand taller. All I have to do now is bring in Charles Darnay. Something the CIA hasn't been able to do for twenty years. Piece of cake, right?

Chapter 11

I swallow the last bite of the cookie I found in the plane's small kitchen, wishing that Kimberly were here. But according to Pete, she's on her honeymoon. Good for her, not as great for us.

Clarity sits beside me, nose stuck deep in her book.

Across the aisle, Truly is asleep, having crashed almost as soon as we got on the plane. Her head rests on Royal's shoulder, her pale blonde hair falling in her face. My dad sits up straight, not daring to move for fear of waking her. Instead, he's reading something on his phone, his entire body stiff but for his thumb, which he's using to scroll down his screen. Truly is doing remarkably well, despite having been dragged into this and out of the relative safety of her brownstone back in D.C.

Haru sits in the seat in front of Truly, trying to calm Baron, who doesn't appear to be a fan of flying. The cat is distracted, constantly whipping around to confirm that, yes, he's still in a strange place with strange people, his bushy tail flicking through the air. Once he's taken another long look around the plane, he returns his focus to Haru, who is crooning sweet cat-nothings in a low voice. Baron bats at Haru's face, and then leaps down from his perch to stalk toward the back of the plane.

In the row in front of Clarity and me, Julep and Lotus are whispering, their heads together. He's got one of her hands wrapped in his own. Whatever he says seems to bolster her. Then he stands and rejoins Pete in the cockpit.

I have to admit that Lotus and Julep seem to work really well together, much like how I felt I was meshing with a certain other teammate. Memories of all the time I spent with Starling in Palermo come unbidden to the front of my mind: the fancy restaurant, dancing the night away with Melina Arnoni, the party at her grandfather's house the night we rescued Clarity. The fake/real kiss we shared. I push the thoughts away. I can't dwell on our past. I need to focus on the present, on getting this job done before anyone else gets hurt.

After that, there's so much I'll have to do as the team's new official leader, including finding a new place to call home. I probably won't have time to worry about such trivial things as relationships. Look at Royal. He's been so busy since Clarity and I were little, he's just now dating. But the curl in my gut makes a liar out of me. If this thing with Starling doesn't work out, if he turns out to be a traitor, it's going to hit me hard. I shove the weighty thought away.

"Hey," I whisper, tapping the side of my sister's leg with the back of my hand. "I've been thinking about what I want our new home base to be like. I'm thinking maybe something above ground, like an old factory building or something, outside of the hubbub of D.C. I'm picturing large windows, at least on the upper floors, motion sensor-detecting lasers, maybe our own private runway…" I trail off when I realize that Clarity has hunched down farther in her seat at my words, withdrawing into herself. "What's wrong?" I ask, leaning toward her.

Her eyes meet mine, large and shiny, pleading with me in

silence.

I lean toward her. "What is it?"

She takes a deep breath to steady herself, and then speaks. "I've been thinking about it too, what I want to do after this mission is over."

"And?"

She pulls her bottom lip into her mouth with her teeth. "I want to apply to the New York School of Costume Design and Special Effects Makeup."

My heart drops. "Oh." I don't know what else to say. I knew Clarity didn't want to work in the field anymore as a spy, but I assumed she'd stay on as our disguise coordinator. It never occurred to me that she'd want to do something else entirely.

"Are you mad?" The words are so quiet, I consider pretending I didn't hear them at all. She continues, a little louder. "You're mad."

Honestly, I am a little mad. Clarity is single-handedly throwing a giant wrench in the plans I had for our future. I thought we would work for the CIA together, kicking butt and taking down the bad guys. It's what I wanted for us. But I can't tell her so. She's always been a great listener, encouraging, supportive of my dream of being a master spy. The least I can do is give her the same courtesy.

I let out a tension-relieving sigh. "No, I'm not mad. This isn't what I was expecting, but I understand." I meet her eyes, willing my face to convey support rather than frustration. It must work, because she throws her arms around me and hugs me tight.

"Thank you," she says before leaning back. "I'll still help you find the perfect place, okay? One with actual windows." Her lips curve up into a teasing smile.

"That'll be great." But without my sister, will it be great, really?

Chapter 12

Royal gets out of his seat, stretches, and comes to stand at the edge of my seat. Meeting Clarity's eyes, he speaks. "Would you give us a minute? I need to talk to your sister."

Clarity's eyes widen as she glances at me, but she climbs over me and goes to sit in the vacated chair next to Truly. Our former teacher smiles over at her, leaning close and saying something I can't hear. Clarity blushes in response.

Royal takes Clarity's seat and levels a serious look at me. "I know I said I was retiring and leaving you in charge, but there are a couple of things we have to talk about first."

My pulse increases and I fidget with my hands, wondering what he could possibly have to talk to me about. Maybe he's about to divulge some of the secrets I know he's kept from us over the years? Trade secrets? How he arranges our jobs? Suddenly I'm very much looking forward to this conversation. There's so much I can learn from him, still, and I'm eager to get started. "I do have some questions. How do you arrange for jobs? It's not like we can advertise. Also, do you have any tips for finding a new home base? I was thinking something above ground…" My words falter at the grim line of my dad's mouth. Clearly, these types of things are not the topics he had in mind when he came to sit beside me.

He clears his throat, his adam's apple bobbing. "You know my thoughts on fraternization among teammates." I start to roll my eyes, and he holds up a hand to stop me. "Just hear me out. You can't deny that with Starling absent, you've spent a lot of time wondering if he's really a traitor, if there were signs that you missed. If you let your emotions get in the way."

My blood chills. It's as if he's read my very thoughts. "How do you know all of that?"

Royal's head tilts. "You're my daughter. And you aren't exactly subtle."

"Fair point."

"I know you don't agree with my policy on this, but I think you can agree that your feelings for Starling are clouding your thoughts, which is exactly why I have this rule in the first place. Getting involved with another spy is messy, and it almost never ends well. It's why I think you should transfer Julep to another office."

My mouth drops open. Transfer Julep? Where to? It's not like there are cells like ours all over the U.S., are there? But as the thought occurs to me, I strike it down. Of course there are. We aren't the only spies employed by the CIA. And it explains why all of our jobs have been in the eastern portion of the country. How stupid could I be? Still, I don't know if I can bring myself to send Julep away. Lotus would be pissed. And I would miss her steadying presence. My stomach clenches. My dad might be right. I've dug myself into a hole by allowing the two of them to date in secret, and now I don't see a way out that doesn't end up with at least one person on my team being reassigned. I push my eyes up to meet my dad's, despite the tears of frustration that threaten.

The corners of his mouth lift in an empathetic smile. "I'm

sorry. I know it's difficult. I think you'll see in time that it's the right course of action. I'll tell her." He begins to rise from the seat.

"Wait. No. Let me think about it some more before we tell them something like that. It can wait until we're done with this job, can't it?"

Royal purses his lips, but gives a curt nod. "All right." He returns to his seat, sending Clarity back over to her spot beside me. She smiles at me as she taps my shoulder with her own. "I like Truly. Don't you? And it's obvious that Dad's crazy about her. Don't you think?"

I bite my lip, unable to deny the warm look that passes between them when our dad takes his seat. Still, I'm not in the mood for nattering about having a potential step mom. Taking a breath to prevent my words from coming out too harshly, I speak. "Not now, okay?"

She studies me with narrowed eyes for a moment, then relaxes into her seat. "I guess it's not the best time."

My head tilts to the side as if to say, "You think?"

Clarity's face grows serious again. "There's something else I wanted to ask you about." She bites her bottom lip, her large brown eyes shimmering as she looks at me.

"Okay…"

Taking a deep breath, she speaks, her calm voice belied by the way she's twisting her fingers in her lap. "I've been thinking about Uncle Nestore, and the ambush at the airport…"

"Don't say it."

"What if he didn't know about it?"

I sigh, not altogether surprised. Clarity's such a positive person. She always wants to believe the best of people, but in this case, it's a recipe for heartache.

"I don't see how they could have traced your phone

without him knowing about it. I just don't think it's very likely."

My sister's eyes fall to her lap, her long, dark lashes feathering over her cheeks. "But is it possible?"

"I guess... if they somehow installed an app on his phone without his knowledge, then used it to trace your location while he was talking to you... But it sounds a little far fetched, don't you think?"

She turns her face up toward mine. "It's just that I was finally getting to know some of my mom's family. I was excited to visit them, once we're done with this job. I could have seen where I came from, my roots. Maybe even gotten to know more about my mom."

Reaching over, I take her hand and give her fingers a squeeze. "I know, and I'm sorry about the whole thing. But I don't think you should contact him again, at least not for a while."

Clarity huffs. "I want to ask him if he knew they were coming for me. Don't you think I have the right to know? I can't live wondering if they're going to try to hurt me again. That's part of the reason I want to quit. I want to be able to go out and about with worrying about being shot at or kidnapped." She shakes her head.

The despair in her voice tugs at something in me, and I find myself speaking, against my better judgment. "Hey. If you want to call him to see what he says after all this is over, use a burner phone. And once you're done, toss it."

"I know how to use a burner phone," she says. "Thanks."

"Any time."

My sister leans over me toward the window. "Mind if we switch places? I'd like to look out for a while."

"Sure." I scoot into her seat as she scrabbles over me into the place I've vacated. Then, she leans against the window and burrows down into her bulky cream-colored sweater, looking perfectly content, despite everything.

Goosebumps rise on my arms. The plane cabin is cold, all of a sudden. I tighten the belt on my trenchcoat and pop the collar, hoping it'll help. Then, I put in my headphones, turn up my music, and close my eyes, willing my thoughts to cease swirling.

Chapter 13

Once our plane is on the ground in Georgia, we circle up at the back of the cabin for a meeting before rushing off to Julep's grandmother's house.

Beyond the plane's windows, darkness has descended over the airport. Blue lights line the runway, illuminating it for use by the next plane. It's a cloudless night, and stars twinkle in the navy canopy. I almost wish it were cloudy, that the moon's light was blotted out. It would make our approach to the house where Julep's grandmother lives easier. It might give us the element of surprise, if Darnay has some of his Cobalt Security forces stationed there, like I expect.

"I've gone back over the satellite footage," Haru says from her seat, spinning her laptop around to show an aerial view of a small home behind a Dairy Queen. "The only movement has been a woman who came by earlier this afternoon and stayed for a couple of hours."

"It was probably my grandma's nurse. She comes three times a week to check up on her, do light cleaning, that kind of thing." Julep fidgets in her seat, unable to still her hands. I don't blame her. If I had a grandma I was close to who might be in danger, I'd be inclined to go in with guns blazing and ask questions later. But that's not Royal's style at all, and, honestly, once I'm truly in charge of the team, I probably should cease all blazing and focus on strategizing instead. I roll my shoulders to rein in my focus on what my dad is saying.

"Julep and Lotus will go into the house first and make sure that it's secure. Clarity and I will be waiting at the perimeter in case they need assistance. Loveday, you will—"

"Stay with Haru. Yeah, yeah." I shift my injured leg, testing it, and am punished by a wince of pain. "Stupid leg," I mutter.

Beside me, Clarity squeezes my uninjured knee. "You'll be good as new in no time," she whispers.

"Not soon enough."

"As I was saying," Royal continues, shooting me a warning look to quash any impulses I have to interrupt further, "once Julep and Lotus have secured the house, Clarity and I will move in to sweep the grounds. At that point, we'll meet inside to regroup."

"We're all clear that this is probably a trap, right?" Lotus says, scanning all of us.

"Obviously," I say.

"But we don't have a choice," Julep says. "We can't leave my grandma alone if Mr. Darnay is coming here to hurt her. I won't stand for it, y'all."

Lotus takes her hand, which causes my dad to stiffen where he stands.

I push up to a stand, leaning on my good leg, before he gets the chance to chastise them. "We aren't going to let anything happen to her, all right? I promised no more losses, and I meant it. Even though I'm injured, I'll do everything I can to make sure all of us get out of this unscathed."

Haru frowns, shoulders sagging. "I wish I still had the

drone. I could be more help."

"We'll get you a new one, as soon as we can."

She smiles up at me, encouraged.

As if he approves of my words, Baron rubs against my leg. But when I bend down to give him a pat, he hisses up at me with those acid yellow eyes and skirts away.

Our vehicle moves in and out of the circles of light pooled on the road without sound. I breathe deeply as I lean against the window, letting the outside world pass by in a haze without really looking at any of it.

Julep tugs at her hair, unable to sit still. Her grandma still isn't answering her phone.

Clarity slings her arm over Julep's shoulder and pulls her closer. "She's going to be okay," my sister says in a low, calming voice.

Julep purses her lips, but doesn't argue. For her sake, I hope Clarity is right.

Lotus jabs at my leg with an outstretched finger. "Hey."

"Ow! What was that for?" My eyes rise to meet his.

"I've been thinking about why Starling didn't tell the rest of us about his dad. You know?"

I glance toward the front of the vehicle, where Royal is driving. I lick my lips. "He didn't tell me either."

His brows knit together. "What do you mean?"

I lean my head back against the headrest. "You remember after the mud run, when Darnay showed up at the Tower?"

"Yeah."

"I was suspicious—"

"Like always."

I chuckle. "Right, so I bugged the control room."

"You did not." The glow from a streetlight flashes through the window, illuminating the incredulous look on Lotus's face for a moment before he is again shrouded in darkness.

"I did, and I overheard Darnay talking to Starling. That's when I found out. He didn't tell me either."

Lotus's head bobs. "I have a theory about that. What if he didn't tell you who he was because he was working with his dad the whole time? Like a double agent. Or a mole."

I'm already shaking my head.

"Think about it. It's pretty shady, him not telling us."

"I bet Royal ordered him not to tell us. You know how he is about us sharing personal information."

His head inclines to one side. "Yeah, but this is kind of a big thing not to share. It's not like any of the rest of us are related. Except for you and Royal, of course." And Clarity, but he still doesn't know that.

Shit. I am like my dad, keeping secrets from my fellow teammates.

The car slows, and I peer out the windshield toward the street ahead. We're almost to the location Royal picked as our staging area.

Now is not the time, but once this is over, I'll shed some of the secrets I carry, but unlike a blood-letting of old, hopefully it'll bring healing rather than weakness.

Chapter 14

Haru, Truly, and I watch from the van we've parked in the alley as Julep, Lotus, Royal, and Clarity advance toward the house where Julep's grandma lives. The wooden fence is weather-stained but sturdy, and the garbage cans are lined up neatly near the back gate. An arch covered in thorny bougainvillea beckons them through into the elderly woman's yard. Mercifully, it doesn't squeak as the four of them move into the darkened space beyond.

I take a deep breath as they disappear behind the fence. It's tall enough that I can't see anything beyond, aside from the eaves and roofline of the small cottage. Above, the moon shines down on the shingles, washing them in silver light.

Outside the car, the night is still. No breeze rustles the leaves of the trees. No cars move along the streets. Even the Dairy Queen is closed at this hour, or I'd be tempted to get some ice cream to pass the time. At least then I'd have something to do.

"We're moving toward the back of the house," Royal says through the comms. "It appears there's a television on inside. It's the only light source, as far as I can see."

Footsteps slide over the grass, their faint sounds

emanating through my earbud.

Truly looks at me, a question in her eyes, and I give her a thumbs up. I'd give her my earbud, but I can't. I have to be able to hear whatever's going on inside the house, just in case my teammates need me. My fingers hover over the gun at my waist, drawing comfort from the fact that we were able to stop at a gun store and replenish our ammo. If this is a trap set by Darnay, and my money is on the fact that it is, at least we'll be able to defend ourselves.

I tap my fingers on my thighs, willing my teammates to move quickly. The suspense is killing me.

"I don't see anyone inside," Royal says. "Julep, Lotus, proceed. Clarity and I will check the outside perimeter."

"Yes, sir."

Several quiet clicking sounds reach my ears. It's Lotus picking the lock on the back door. He's not as good at it as I am, but he manages. "We're moving inside," he whispers.

My breaths reverberate in my ears. If this is an ambush, Royal made it clear that I was to get Haru and Truly to safety. I list my hands and wrap my fingers around the steering wheel, hoping it doesn't come to that. If it does, I'm not sure I'll have the strength to leave the rest of my family inside. But I'll have to, no matter what.

A yowling sound cuts through the night, making me whip my head around, drawing my gun in steady hands.

Haru squeaks in fright, and Truly's gaze follows mine. She sags in relief. "It's just a cat," she whispers, pointing. "At the other end of the alley. See it?"

My eyes strain to see. There it is. A hunched figure flickers across the alley and recedes into the shadows on the other side.

We're all a little jumpy.

"Lotus, on me," Julep whispers over the comms.

"Yes, ma'am."

Another minute expands in the silence. I focus on their words almost silent footsteps as they sweep the house, straining my ears to hear any noises that are out of place.

Julep's voice comes. "The house is clear. There isn't anyone here."

"Affirmative," Royal responds. "Clarity and I are coming inside."

"I'm going to check on my grandma," Julep says. I hear the snap of her gun being secured in its holster. "It appears this wasn't a trap at all."

Haru taps at her keyboard. "But then why would Mr. Darnay come to Georgia? He doesn't have any properties here."

My eyebrows rise. Frankly, I'm shocked that this hasn't evolved into a firefight. We've certainly had our fair share of those over the past few days. Why *would* Darnay come to Georgia, if not for Julep's grandma?

Royal's voice interrupts my thoughts. "Loveday, please escort Haru and Truly into the house."

I reach over and pat the side of the front passenger seat where Truly is sitting. "It's safe to go inside now."

She swivels to look back at me. "Thanks."

We get out of the car and I motion for Haru and Truly to go ahead of me. They move quietly through the back gate. I turn to check the alley one more time, gun at the ready. I don't see movement anywhere, not even that mangy cat. I wait, just in case. There's nothing. I step backward through the gate, latching it behind me, and jog as best I can with my crutch to catch up with Haru and Truly as they open the back door and are ushered into the house by Lotus.

"Grandma? Are you okay?" Julep asks from the front of

the house.

"This way," Lotus says, gesturing toward the door at the far side of the kitchen.

We walk through to find Julep crouched over a tan reclining chair, the blue light from the television flickering over her as she peers down at the elderly woman asleep in the chair. The woman's head is reclined against the headrest, her eyes closed. Her mouth gapes, and a quiet snore escapes.

I lift my hand to cover my smiling mouth.

"Grandma?" Julep asks, shaking the older woman's arm gently.

The woman snorts and startles awake, blinking up at Julep through her thick glasses. "Nia? Is that you?"

Julep grins. "Yes, grandma. It's me. I came to visit you."

I step back into the shadows, Haru and Truly at my back, to make sure that Julep's grandma cannot see us. Lotus, Royal, and Clarity are positioned behind the older woman's reclining chair, the hallway at their backs in case they need to vacate the room in a hurry.

"It's been too long. Shame on you, girl, for not visiting your old grandma. I'm almost out of socks." By way of proof, she lifts her feet to reveal hand-knitted, multi-colored socks. One of them has a hole through which the woman's big toe protrudes. "Do you know how cold my feet get in these things?"

Julep gives a pleased laugh and pulls a brand new pair of socks out of her belt. "I brought you these. I know how much you like purple and red."

Her grandma grabs at the socks eagerly. "Oh, they're pretty. And so soft." She kicks at her feet. "Help me get these old things off, will you?"

"I'm going to get a glass of water," Truly whispers. At my

nod, she moves back toward the kitchen.

"Yes, ma'am," Julep says, kneeling to exchange the old socks for new ones. "There you go. Good as new."

Behind me, a kitchen cabinet door swings open with a squeak.

"What's that?" Julep's grandma asks, swiveling toward the sound.

Lotus and the others step backward into the darkened hallway.

"I didn't hear anything," Julep says with a shrug. "Shall we get you to bed? It's late."

Grandma smacks her lips. "I guess so. After all the tea I've had today. I told the nice Englishman that I preferred iced tea to hot, but he insisted I try it. It was too hot."

My blood runs cold as she goes on about her tea.

"Englishman?" Haru whispers in my ear.

I nod, turning to face the back of the house, and motion for her to get behind me.

"An Englishman came to visit you? Who was he?" Julep asks, her tone remarkably calm.

"Oh, a nice gentleman. I've seen him on TV. He came to visit me today. Such a charming man."

Royal, Clarity, and Lotus retreat down the hallway and step into the kitchen. "Fan out," Royal says. "They could still be here."

"Royal?" Truly's voice is shaky as she holds up a thin sheet of paper in a trembling hand.

My dad steps toward her and takes the paper from her hand.

"Here," Lotus says, lighting up the flashlight on his watch.

Royal squints as he reads the note. "It's from Charles. He wants me to meet him in the Philippines, at the park where

Maureen was killed. Alone."

"That's not happening," I whisper, my voice rough. "We're not sending you like a lamb to slaughter."

"Tell her the rest," Truly prompts, her voice cracking.

"There's more?" Clarity asks, eyes wide in the gloom.

Royal shifts his weight. "I have one day to meet him there, or Charles will start killing one agent every 24 hours until I appear."

"Well, shit," I whisper, running my fingers through my hair.

"You can't go, Dad. He'll kill you." Clarity pleads with him. She holsters her gun and puts a hand on his arm. "Please don't go."

Royal puts a hand over hers. "I don't have a choice. I won't allow innocent agents to be murdered if I can stop it."

She shakes her head. "You can't leave us alone."

"You won't be alone."

She huffs, not saying anything else.

Above me, something shifts in the attic. At least I assume the house has an attic, based on the arched roofline and the standard height ceilings. I raise my gun to point toward the sound and go still, listening.

"Did you hear that?" Lotus rasps.

"Shh," I hiss, straining my ears.

There it is again. Something shifts in the attic above, and it's too large to be a mouse or rat.

"Where is the attic access?" I whisper.

Lotus motions down the hallway.

I gesture for him to take the lead, and follow along the unlit space. My pulse speeds as I grip my gun. Whoever is in the attic is in for a surprise.

Truly and Haru tuck themselves in behind me, and Royal

and Clarity bring up the rear.

Julep's pleasant voice wafts after us from the living room, where she's still talking to her grandma.

Lotus stops at the end of the hall and points up toward the ceiling.

If I squint, I can just make out a square cutout in the popcorn ceiling.

Footsteps shuffle over the ceiling above, moving nearer to the hatch.

Putting my finger to my lips, I beckon everyone to be quiet. I push Truly and Haru into the bathroom and point toward the tub, hoping they catch my meaning. Then I close the door on them. If we have to start shooting, the tub may provide some protection, assuming it's steel or cast-iron.

The rest of us line the hallway, Lotus nearest the hatch, followed by Royal, Clarity, and then me. We wait, weapons at the ready, for whoever is up in the attic to show themselves.

I swallow, standing on my one good foot.

Slowly, the attic hatch inches open.

I take in a silent breath. Is it Charles Darnay? But I don't think so. Hiding in a dusty attic doesn't seem like his style.

An aluminum folding ladder extends down from the opening, its hinges creaking.

My pulse leaps. Here we go.

A boot steps down onto the first rung, and the second boot follows.

My eyes widen in recognition as the figure moves into view. My heart lurches into my throat.

Starling jumps down from the ladder and turns.

Without hesitation, Royal trains his weapon on the boy's chest. "What are you doing here?"

Clarity shudders but doesn't lower her gun.

Starling holds up both hands to show us that he's unarmed. It's a display of surrender.

With a cry of rage, Lotus hauls off and punches him in the jaw.

Chapter 15

Starling staggers backward, wiping at the blood that dribbles out of his mouth.

"I'm gonna kill you!" Lotus yells, pulling back his fist for another punch.

There's a yelp of surprised fear from the living room.

"Shh," I whisper-yell at Lotus.

"What's going on?" Julep yells, pushing past me with arms outstretched.

But I beat her to it. With a sweep of my crutch, I pull Lotus's feet out from under him with a satisfying whoosh. He falls flat on his back on the carpet, the wind knocked out of him. His hands flop onto his chest as he tries to catch his breath. Angry daggers shoot from his eyes as he peers up at me.

"Nia? What's going on back there?" Julep's grandma calls in a shaky voice.

"It's okay, Grandma. Somehow the TV in the guest room got turned on to a crime show."

"It sounds terrible."

"Yeah it does." She levies a wary look at me.

"Sorry." I step over Lotus, my heart pounding as I approach Starling. There are so many different things I want to say to him right now, in this moment. Anger, confusion, and relief war within my chest.

Starling doesn't move as I draw near to him, his brown eyes locked on mine.

I hesitate for a second, then fling my arms around him, pressing my cheek into his chest. My crutch clatters to the ground. "You're safe."

Clarity gasps.

"What the hell?" Lotus gasps out.

Starling pats my back before taking my arms in his sturdy hands and putting me away from him. "I'm safe." His gaze flicks over my head to the rest of the team, behind me. "I suppose I should explain, if you'll allow it."

There's a beat of silence.

I turn around to face them—Royal, Clarity, Lotus, Julep, Haru, and Truly. Their expressions run the gamut from rage to shock and back again.

"Julep, take his weapon," Royal orders, his gun still pointed at Starling's heart.

Julep's eyes flick from Royal to me, and my heart swells at her loyalty. That kind of trust can't be bought. I give her a slight nod. "It's okay. Do as he says."

With bunched eyebrows, Julep complies, taking the handgun from the holster at Starling's waist and stepping back to hand it to Royal. Reaching down, she gives Lotus a hand up, and the two of them stand facing us. Lotus rubs at the knuckles on his hand, still scowling.

Starling leans down and, retrieving my crutch from the floor, hands it to me.

"Thanks."

"You knew, this whole time that he was on our side," Clarity says, her eyes piercing me with reproach.

I shrug. "I did. We had to make his defection look real, or Darnay would know."

"I'm so sorry, everyone," Starling says, his voice imbued with sincerity.

Finally, Royal lowers his weapon, though he doesn't holster it. "Let's move in there, shall we?" He indicates the back bedroom with a lift of his chin. "Julep, go tuck in your grandma, all right? Then join us in here, so Starling can explain what exactly is going on."

She nods and scurries up the hall to where the faint sounds of a game show are emanating from the television.

The rest of us shuffle into what turns out to be a guest bedroom. I try to ignore the stiff looks my teammates are giving me, especially my sister.

Squinting through the darkness in the back of the painter's van, I check on my teammates. Clarity has fallen asleep with her tablet in her lap. Haru is also out, with Baron stretched out beside her, and Truly is still sleeping as well. Up front, Lotus is focused on the road ahead, and Royal is consulting his phone. Julep is in the passenger seat, her eyes closed and her head bouncing against the headrest every time the van drives over a pothole in the road.

"Hey," I whisper to Starling, the only other person who's awake back here. "Can I talk to you for a minute?"

He looks over at me from where he's sitting at the edge of the makeshift mattress I'm lying on. I prop myself up against the side of the vehicle, despite the metal bolt that digs into my back.

"What can I do for you?" Starling whispers, scooting closer to me. He takes my hand, enveloping my fingers in the soft warmth of his skin. There are calluses on his fingers from shooting a gun that are similar to the rough spots on my own hands.

I send a furtive glance toward Clarity, but she appears to be sleeping still. "You aren't going to like it."

"I'll do it anyway, if you ask."

My heart pounds at the earnest timbre of his voice. He's telling me the truth. I know he'll comply with whatever I'm about to say. For the first time, I want to balk at having that kind of power over another person. But still I push ahead. "It has to be a secret. We can't tell anyone. Darnay has to believe it."

His eyes widen in understanding, and the whites of his eyes stand out in the shadows. "You want me to pretend to double cross your team and join my father?"

I nod. "It's the only way. If you're with your—Darnay, you'll be able to keep tabs on him and let me know what's going on. We'll be able to get a step ahead. Theoretically."

He's remains still for so long I'm positive he's going to refuse me, despite his earlier words. I know what it is I'm asking of him. Not only will he be putting himself in serious danger of physical harm, he'll be setting fire to the bridges he's built with the rest of our team. It's possible he'll never regain the easy camaraderie he has with everyone, if he comes back at all.

Clarity jolts awake, her hair fanning out behind her head.

Starling drops my hand and spins toward her, alert.

Clarity's eyes land on us, and her features rearrange in an uncomfortable smile. "Sorry. Am I interrupting something?"

"No," I blurt.

All three of us laugh uneasily, glancing between each other.

Clarity obviously doesn't believe me, because she puts her wireless headphones. "Okay... I think I'll listen to some music." Faint notes waft from her headphones.

I wait, watching my sister to see if her eyes find us again, but she remains focused on her tablet.

I relax my muscles, allowing my eyes to find Starling's once more.

Our gazes lock, and my heart starts pounding so loudly in my chest that I'm not sure how he doesn't hear it.

The corner of his mouth lifts in a smile. With a tentative hand, he reaches to caress my cheek. I can't help myself; I lean into the touch, relishing his warmth on my skin.

"I'll go."

"Are you sure? It'll be dangerous."

He nods. "There's just one thing I'd like to do first." Starling sends a surreptitious glance toward my sister, and then leans down, inching his face toward mine. Our lips meet, gently at first, then more fervently. I snake my arms around his neck to draw him closer to me, yearning for the press of his solid, sturdy frame against my own. He wraps his arms around me, careful not to bump my injured leg, and holds me close. Long seconds pass before I have to come up for air.

"Wow," he breathes into my neck.

"Yeah." I draw back, meeting his eyes. "So, when Royal sends someone for the next task, you'll volunteer?"

"I will."

"Thank you."

He nods.

"And one more thing: don't die, okay?"

Chapter 16

I can still hear Starling's chuckle as I look around at all of my teammates. "So that's how it happened." I had told them everything about our conversation in the back of the painter's van, on the drive to Dr. Faraday's house. Well, all except for the kissing part. Royal, especially, does not need to know about that part.

I shift my weight in the small recliner I've claimed in the corner of the room, and glance at each of them to gauge their reactions.

Clarity, Julep, and Haru are seated on the edge of the bed, their eyes focused on me like those of a parent on a child who has disappointed them. It's a look I'm not altogether unfamiliar with.

Clarity sighs. "I'm getting tired of all of the secrets."

Julep nods in agreement, but Haru bites her lip as she runs a hand over Baron's silky fur. "I don't know. It kind of makes sense that they didn't tell us. If it were me, I wouldn't have been able to pretend that I thought Starling had left us, so I can understand why they did it that way…" Haru trails off at the sharp look Lotus gives her.

"I'm with Clarity," Lotus says, voice tight. "The secrets

have to go." He leans back against the wall, hands shoved into his pockets.

I chew my lip, glancing at Starling where he stands near the closed door before meeting Royal's gaze. He tilts his head as if saying, "This is your team now. Do as you please." But in my mind, I remember all of the times he insisted that we keep information to ourselves to protect our teammates. It's like having an honest Royal on one shoulder, and a cautious one on the other, each whispering into one of my ears. The silence stretches out as I debate within myself. What should I do?

I look at each of my teammates, all of whom are waiting to see what I'll say. Finally, I sit up straight as much as I can in the old, soft chair. "I agree. No more secrets. From here on out, we share whatever information we find out, and we plan together, as a unit." I focus on Starling. "Can you bring us up to date on your father's whereabouts?"

"And tell us what you're doing here," Lotus mumbles, rubbing at his bruised knuckles.

Starling stands at attention. "As to what I'm doing here: my father sent me to deliver the message for Royal. I assume you found the written note in the kitchen?"

Truly nods. "I found it."

"I'm surprised he'd leave a written note instead of a body, like his previous message."

Starling purses his lip. "He intended to leave another… individual… but the men he sent to retrieve another hostage came back empty handed. He decided to send a handwritten note because it would be easier to destroy than a digital message."

"True. As they say, the internet is forever," I deadpan.

Lotus shifts where he stands, his movements edged with tension. "You're telling us that he let you cruise in here by yourself with a note?" He cocks an eyebrow in unabashed disbelief.

"Well…" Starling's eyes dart toward mine. Whatever he's about to say, it's not good news. "He told me to leave the note, then fall back to wait until your group arrived. He ordered me to kidnap one of you to assure that Royal would come to the rendezvous point, as requested. He suggested it wouldn't be hard to capture Truly or Haru while the rest of you were assessing the house."

At this, Truly shrinks toward Royal, gripping his arm.

"I won't let him take you," my dad says to her in a low voice.

She murmurs something in response, not letting go of him.

Clarity's eyebrows rise in surprise. "He's that angry?"

Starling nods. "He's furious."

Royal scrubs at the stubble on his jaw. "I can't believe it's come to this. I've known Charles for twenty five years…"

"Did you really kill his wife?" Lotus asks. "That's what he said back in the Tower."

Royal lowers his gaze to the floor. "I did. I was told that there was a wanted terrorist harboring in the Philippines. They sent me down there alone to eliminate her. The morning of the shooting, they sent me her location and a description. I took up position on top of a nearby building…" He looks up to meet Starling's gaze. "I saw her at the park, watching a little boy. According to the intelligence, she didn't have any family, so I thought perhaps she was acting as a babysitter or nanny. I didn't know she was your mother. I waited until the little boy was on top of the slide, a sufficient distance from the target, and then I pulled the trigger."

Starling closes his eyes and draws a ragged breath.

"There must have been a mistake somewhere," I say. "The CIA wouldn't order you to eliminate some random woman, or even less, someone married to an MI6 officer."

Royal nods. "I've thought it over, and that's the conclusion I came to as well. But it doesn't make it any less painful for Charles, and Starling here."

I shake my head. Nothing could make the loss of a loved one less painful. In fact, if I found out that my mother was accidentally killed by an agent on a mistaken order, it might even make it worse. I can't imagine what Starling must be feeling right now, knowing that his mother's death was a fluke. Taking it further, I can kind of understand why Darnay is so angry, even if I don't agree with his methods.

"You guys don't think he'll really kill someone every 24 hours until you surrender, do you?" Lotus asks, swiping at the back of his neck with a rough hand. "That seems pretty intense."

Everything I know about Darnay flicks through my mind like a classic television clip show, from our first introduction to our conversation in the Tower mere days ago. Then I recall the story my dad told us about the attacks on agents twenty years ago, all of the agents who lost their lives, in Darnay's quest to avenge the tragic death of his wife at my own father's hands. Surety builds in me. "He'll do it. Remember what Royal told us about the attacks twenty years ago? The agents dying in suspicious ways? The CIA thought it was Nexus then, they just didn't know who he was. Now we know."

"You think it was him all this time?" Julep asks, raising her eyes to meet mine.

"I do. Remember what he said about it?"

"He called it a 'nasty business," my sister puts in. "Now that I think about it, did he seem a little proud of it during that conversation to anyone else?"

Haru shudders. "How could anyone be proud of killing innocent people?"

Starling flinches at this, as if he's embarrassed by his father's conduct. "I feel that I should apologize," he grinds out.

His assumption of responsibility is endearing. It's all I can do not to wrap my arms around him again and whisper reassurances in his ear. "None of this is your fault. You have nothing to apologize for."

"Yeah, man, I guess we're good," Lotus says, giving Starling a hard slap on the shoulder.

"What are we going to do?" Clarity asks, tucking one of her long legs underneath her.

I look at each of my teammates, thinking. "I've got a plan, but you're not going to like it."

"What have you got in mind?" Royal asks, a wary look in his eyes.

Footsteps shuffle down the hall, muffled against the carpet. "Nia? Are you still here?"

My eyes fly to the door. We can't let Julep's grandmother catch us in here, much less get a good look at any of us.

But Julep is off the wall and striding toward the door before anyone else has a chance to move. From the looks of it, she's got things under control.

"Happy Halloween," I mutter, but no one hears.

Chapter 17

Julep's voice is a murmur from next door, where she's talking to her grandma as the older woman gets a glass of water and climbs back into bed. Her voice rises and falls like wind chimes tinkling in the breeze on a brisk spring day.

A door closes with a click, and then the door to the guest room swings open. "She's down for the night," Julep says, stepping inside.

"Let's move to the other end of the house," Royal says as he pushes off the wall. Leading Truly by the hand, he treads down the hall in silence and stops in the darkened living room.

"Can we go somewhere we can turn a light on?" Clarity asks as she settles against my shoulder. "All this dark is depressing."

"I agree. Let's go somewhere with lights, and possibly some food." Lotus's stomach growls, bringing a smirk to my face.

"We don't have time for that," I say. "We've wasted too much time already. Darnay is expecting Starling back with a captive, and my guess is he won't take kindly to being kept waiting."

"Agreed," Royal says.

"Which is why I'm going with him," I say, voice firm.

"Absolutely not," my dad says, shaking his head.

"I agree, that's a bad idea," Julep puts in.

"Why can't Starling just tell us where Darnay is hiding, and we can go get him?"

I shake my head. "We need to maintain Starling's cover for as long as we can. If we simply go in there with guns blazing, Darnay will know that Starling was either working with us, or was captured. And he won't take kindly to either. If Starling and I go to him, I think he'll be more stable. He'll have a hostage, and the assurance that Royal will show up in the Philippines."

"I hate to say it, but she's making sense," Lotus says.

"I still don't like it," Royal says.

"We don't have a choice," I say. "I'm not sending Truly or Haru to Darnay. Besides, it's plausible that since I'm injured I'd be kept on the back lines. I'd be much easier to grab than any of the rest of you."

Clarity's hand wraps around mine. "Please don't," she pleads.

My gut clenches. There are so many ways this could go wrong. Darnay could simply decide to kill me in revenge for his wife's death, but I believe one hundred percent that Starling would do his level best to stop him. From what Starling has told me about his relationship with his dad, they aren't close. Maybe not even close enough to protect Starling himself from his father's anger. If that were to happen, we'd both be in trouble, but we'd be in it together. Still, I keep all of that to myself. I don't want my team to know I have reservations about this, because if they do they'll never let me go. And I don't want to think about what will happen then. I'm guessing it would involve more headlines about mutilated bodies, and I can't stand and let innocent people be killed.

"I'm sorry, but I have to. I'll go with Starling. I'll wear a tracker. And once we arrive wherever Darnay is hiding, you can come rescue me and capture Darnay. You'll be big damn heroes."

The corner of Lotus's mouth twitches upward. "That doesn't sound too terrible."

Julep huffs and elbows him in the ribs.

"Ow!"

Royal sighs in resignation. "Where is Charles now?"

"He and the remainder of the men he hired from Cobalt Security are waiting for me at a private landing strip outside of Atlanta. My father paid the owner to stay away for the next several days so he would have exclusive access to the area. The owner agreed once my father mentioned that he was considering building a luxury hotel nearby that would result in more customers at the air strip."

A blur of movement outside the window catches my eye. I stare at it, hackles raised, but don't see anything more. It could have been a cat or possum or something, or nothing at all. This job is making me paranoid.

I clear my throat. "You guys, we have to move. Starling and I will go to the air strip to meet Darnay. Haru, you can keep a lock on my location with my watch, correct?"

"Yes I can! Just don't take it off, and we'll know exactly where you are the whole time."

"Great. Then let's go."

"There's one more thing," Starling says, "before we go."

"What? More intel you can share with us?"

He hesitates. "Not exactly."

Fear coils in my gut. What else could he have to say? Our mission is complicated, and dangerous, enough as it is without adding more on top of the pile.

Starling steps toward me. "My father will be suspicious if I return with you unscathed. I think you should shoot me."

My jaw drops. I was not expecting this.

"I'll shoot him," Lotus is quick to volunteer.

"Shut up," Julep hisses. "No one is shooting anyone."

"Please," Starling says. "Hear me out. If I go back there with Loveday, and I'm not even injured, he may suspect that she came willingly, and we can't have that. He has to believe that I had some difficulty retrieving you."

"Like I said, I'll shoot him. Ouch! Stop hurting me!" Lotus groans as Julep steps on his toes.

"Starling has a point," Royal says, and I know that he's right. They both are. Starling can't go traipsing back to the airfield unscathed, and with me in tow. If Darnay is half as paranoid as I am, he'll be suspicious.

I bite the inside of my cheek. "If you want precision shooting, you need my sister."

Beside me, Clarity's entire body tenses. Her head shakes back and forth. "No, no, no, no. I won't."

I turn to face her through the dark, gripping her arms in my hands. "You have to. You're the best shot, and we can't afford to mess this up."

"I could kill him." The words tremble as they slip past her lips.

"You won't," Starling says confidently. "My father has a medic with him at the air strip, just in case."

"See?"

Clarity crosses her arms. "I'm not shooting anyone. You can't make me." Her every line is harsh as stubborn resolve radiates from her.

I clench my jaw. "Fine. I'll do it."

"We should stage it as a getaway, in case someone is watching," Royal says. "I find it hard to believe that Charles sent Starling here alone. And I fear we've already been inside for too long."

"Smart man."

The air goes cold as the hairs on the back of my neck prickle at the new, unexpected voice. I whip around to face the back door. Four men from Cobalt Security are standing there, weapons trained on us. Then I see the red dots of laser sights on Royal, Julep, Lotus, and myself. Haru and Truly step back, their expressions painted white with fear.

A sharp intake of breath is Starling's only reaction. He wasn't expecting them. Relief floods through me, despite our situation. His reaction is further proof of his loyalty to my team, to me.

I step forward, toward the men, exaggerating my dependency on my crutch. If they underestimate me, it could give our team an advantage, and right now, we need one. The four of them remain where they are, each of their weapons pointed at a different target. "Gentlemen. Nice of you to join us."

"Shut up, girl. And don't come any closer." The man whose gun is pointed at me narrows his eyes.

I halt where I stand, not taking my eyes off the men.

"What are you doing here?" Starling hurls the words, his eyes wide with shock.

The speaker snorts. "You think your dad would let you come here alone? Tsk tsk. And it looks like he was right. It looks to me like you're colluding with the enemy."

Starling's mouth shuts tight.

"Actually, I was just about to shoot him," Lotus says, by way of explanation.

The leader of the Cobalt team eyes him, a disbelieving look in his eye.

My brain whirrs, searching for an angle I can use to talk us out of this, but I scrape the bottom and come up empty.

"Cat got your tongue, chickie?"

I practically snarl at this. "Don't call me that."

He ignores me. "As I was saying. We're under orders to take Royal and the boy back to Mr. Darnay. You'll come with us, nice and slow, or we'll shoot every one of your friends."

Starling recoils.

I grit my teeth, my expression fierce as sparks of anger shoot from my eyes. "That's not going to happen."

The man cocks an eyebrow at me, then turns to Royal. "Come without a fuss, and we won't hurt these infants you call spies."

My mouth curls into a snarl. I am not an infant. And I could probably do more damage with my crutch than these brainless toadies could do with their firearms, if given the element of surprise.

Surprise. That's it.

Royal takes a step toward the men, but I hold out a hand to stop him.

"You guarantee you won't hurt my team?" I ask.

The leader tilts his head, a patronizing grin on his face. "As if you have any leverage, girlie. It looks to me like we've got all of you against a wall. And it wouldn't take more than a slight squeeze…"

"Rocket," one of the other Cobalt guys says in a low voice. "You heard our orders. No killing them. Yet."

Chapter 18

Rocket narrows his eyes. "I just want to shoot them in the same places they shot our boys. They won't die, right away. How about if I shoot this one in the chest, just like they shot Switchback?" He swivels his gun, and the laser sight halts on Baron, whom Haru is clutching to her chest. "Two for one, eh Chopper?"

Chopper grunts. "No shooting."

"Fine," Rocket growls. "You and you, come here." He gestures toward Starling and Royal with the barrel of his gun.

I glance at Clarity, who is shrinking back under the sight of the man's drawn weapon. Then my eyes slide to Royal, who has taken a sure step toward the Cobalt guys. I can't let this happen. I swore to my team we wouldn't lose any more of our loved ones. I have to keep that promise. I won't let them take Royal.

Ignoring the pain in my thigh, I balance my weight on both feet and raise the crutch just a hair, enough for Starling to see the movement. His eye catches mine and holds it for a moment, conveying his understanding of my plan.

I'm prepared to strike. My crutch's metal bars are cold and light in my palms. It won't hold up in an extended fight, so I have to make my first swing count.

At my back, my teammates are frozen, watching and waiting to see what I will do. They know how crucial the element of surprise can be in a situation like this. Without it, we likely wouldn't have a chance.

My heart is pounding as Starling draws level with the two men in the front of the enemy's formation. Without him having to tell me, I anticipate what his next move will be. My grip tightens on my crutch.

Without warning, Starling lunges for the man on the left, Rocket, slamming the edge of his hand down on Rocket's wrist, making him lose his target as the gun barrel swings down to point at the floor.

In a silent, powerful swing, I arc the crutch up under the hands of the man on the right, slamming into the underside of his wrists and forcing them upward toward the popcorn ceiling.

A gunshot shatters the air, and dust rains from above.

From the other bedroom, Julep's grandma screams.

I grit my teeth, hoping she has the sense to stay put and call 911.

Despite the fall temperatures outside, the air in the house is suddenly sweltering. Starling and Rocket are grappling for control of the gun, which is swinging wildly from side to side. They look pretty evenly matched. There is no way to tell who will gain control of the firearm.

"Get down!" I yell without looking over my shoulder at my teammates. I'm trusting that they know enough to keep themselves safe, and in most of their cases, it's true.

"Argh!" Another Cobalt guy grunts as he swings at me with his gun.

I snap my head away from his reach without removing my focus. I can't afford to blink. Adrenaline courses through me as

I bring the crutch upward under the man's flailing arms, ramming the padded top into his abdomen just under his rib cage with every ounce of strength I possess.

He staggers backward, clutching at his stomach. A hole appears dead center in his forehead, and his neck whips back as he falls to the ground with a thud.

Haru's anguished cry pulls me around to glance at her. She's cowering near the floor against the opposite wall, arms wrapped around Truly's legs. Baron is nowhere to be seen.

Clarity stands in the center of the room, gun raised, smoke rising from the barrel. It was she who took down my assailant with a single shot to the skull. It's her first confirmed kill, and from the pained look in her eyes, I can see that it cost her. How much, only time will tell.

"Nobody move," a gruff growl undercuts the chaos as an arm snakes around my waist, yanking me back against the solid body of Chopper. The cold barrel of his gun hits against the side of my head, making pain ricochet around my skull.

Starling and Rocket are locked in a wrestling stance, but Starling's eyes find mine. He gives a slight shake of his head as if to say, "Don't try anything dangerous."

My eyes slide to the rest of my team: Truly and Haru are huddled against the wall. Julep, Lotus, and Royal are standing in a line, holding their firing stance, guns at the ready. And Clarity, is there with arm raised, gun pointed at the third man behind me.

I suck in a breath as fear slithers up my spine. My pulse climbs as I fight to remain in control. Slowly, I drop the crutch and try to lower my center of gravity. If I can just—

"Don't you move," Chopper orders in my ear. "Put your hands behind your back."

My eyes meet Royal's. He locks onto me as the rest of him

remains grounded, unmoving. I look him over, noting the worry lines on his forehead and the gray behind his ears. He's never looked so old as this moment. But I've done what I intended to do. My team won't lose our leader, and father, this day.

My dad's eyes shift to the man holding me hostage. "You're outnumbered. Put down your weapons."

The man holding me snarls. "She'll be dead before you're able to squeeze off a shot." I can feel his body coiled behind my back, his hot breath on the back of my head. Revulsion courses through me at his close proximity, at the pungent scent of his sweat.

Lightning fast, the third man reaches forward and pulls Starling's gun from its holster. Raising it, he holds it to the back of the boy's head.

My gut clenches and I blink. I can't watch them kill another person I love. The realization hits me like a punch to the gut. Starling, this boy standing an arm's length away from me, is someone I love. His eagerness, his efficient capabilities, his boyish charm, his cocky grin. Somehow he's gotten under my skin, peeled back my armor and crawled inside my heart when I wasn't looking.

"Drop your hands," the third man orders, and slowly, Starling complies.

"Everyone stay where you are," Rocket commands, having gained control of his gun once more. "We're walking out of here, and you aren't going to stop us. If you do, we'll kill them." The truth is a naked blade in his hands, slicing through my team, my family, until each of them is left, heart bleeding, staring at us as we retreat toward the back door with controlled steps.

I look around for something, anything I can use as a

weapon, but the odds of me being able to land a blow before Chopper pulls the trigger on the gun aimed right at my head are slim. In minutes, the tables have turned. We're at the mercy of Darnay's hired guns.

In the distance, sirens wail. I hope they're coming for us. Please be coming for us.

We back out the door and down the porch steps as all three of the Cobalt guys remain on high alert, their eyes scanning the house for any sign of movement.

Before I can grasp what's happening, we're in the alley behind the house. The third man secures the gate behind us, keeping his gun raised and ready to shoot at the first sign of any of my team members. I'm half dragged past Dr. Faraday's suburban, and a pit forms in my stomach when i see that the car's tires have been slashed and all of the air spilled out. My team won't be able to use the car to follow us. They'll have to spend time locating another vehicle, and by that time...

I wriggle and fight with all I've got, trying desperately to claw my way out of the muscled arms of the man holding me. If he's going to shoot me, I'd rather go out knowing that I fought with every muscle in my body. Thoughts shoot through my brain like lightning bolts as I take stock of my situation. The man is holding a gun near my temple, and his arms are still snaked around me, holding me pressed against his front. My elbows are useless. I steel myself, swing my good leg forward, then slam it backward into the man's shin, making solid contact. He grunts in pain, but his arm don't loosen. I try kicking again, but the man squeezes his arm into my gut, making my stomach lurch.

"Ow!"

"Don't hurt her!" Starling bellows from behind me. The sounds of struggling begin. Shoes scuffle over the asphalt.

Starling groans in frustration. There's a thump, and all goes quiet.

My heart leaps into my throat. "Starling, are you okay?"

"Yes," he breathes, sounding as if he's gotten the air knocked out of him.

We're pushed toward an armored van, and I renew the struggle. If they get me in there, they could take me anywhere. I've seen the true crime documentaries and know the statistics. Once a kidnapper moves his victim to a secondary location, it's lights out.

I kick the man again with all the force I can muster, pleased when he yowls in pain.

Cold metal slams against my temple, making my head spin as pain cracks through my skull. My eyes water and tears spill onto my cheeks. I grit my teeth to force myself to stop crying. I won't let them see my weakness.

The back doors of the armored car swing open from the inside. A fourth man hurries away to the front of the van and climbs into the driver seat. He fires up the engine. "Let's go," he calls.

I'm tossed roughly into the back of the vehicle. My body slams against the cold metal flooring on my injured leg, making my eyes water once more. I bite my tongue, forcing the tears to recede.

Starling is pushed in after me, his body sliding over the slick floor.

I push upright into a squat, preparing to jump to my feet.

"Go ahead, do it." The hard voice catches my attention, and I look up as the doors slam shut.

Rocket has his gun trained on me, and Chopper and the third man are crouched inside the doors, locking them in place. My crutch is nowhere to be seen. It must have been left behind in the house.

    We're trapped.

Chapter 19

Outside, my teammates shout demands that we be set free, but they fall on deaf ears.

"Don't let them leave," Royal roars.

Gunshots pelt against the windows in the front of the van, to no avail.

"Get us out of here," Rocket orders, somehow still calm despite the melee.

"Yes, sir." The driver slams on the gas, and the vehicle barrels forward through the narrow alley like a bull in a china shop. It rams an empty garbage can, which tumbles forward into the street, banging loudly against the concrete as it rolls.

The sirens draw closer, but not fast enough.

The armored car careens around the corner and away into the night.

Slowly, I lower myself to the floor and ease my hands behind my back.

"Stop moving," Rocket says. "Search them."

I glare, hunching against the wall that separates the cargo area from the cab. "Don't touch me."

"Boss's orders," Rocket says, amusement playing on his features.

My stomach churns as the third man crosses the cargo area and pulls me up roughly by the arm.

Burning pain shoots up my leg, but I bite back the cry that threatens to break from my throat. I won't give them that satisfaction.

The third man is quick, but thorough, using his immaculate hands to make sure I'm not hiding anything useful where it can't be seen. I shut off my emotions and pretend I'm standing in line at the airport, allowing a TSA agent to check me over before I board a plane. It feels about as impersonal, though I'm much more annoyed when the man takes my earbud, watch, gun, and utility belt, leaving me with nothing but the clothes I'm wearing.

"Your shoes too," he orders.

I snarl. "You can't have my shoes."

He huffs and unholsters his gun. Pointing it at my chest, he repeats the command.

"Fine. Buttwipe." This last I mumble, not sure how he'll react to name-calling. For the first time, a flicker of fear kindles in my belly, like a lit candle glowing on a dark night. I untie my shoes and toss them to him. So much for having the laces to work with. The man chucks them deftly into the front seat, along with the rest of the confiscated items, minus my handgun. That he pockets in an interior coat pocket. I clench my jaw in frustration.

The one item he doesn't toss into the front seat is my watch. Instead, with one precise motion, he puts the device on the metal floor and stomps on it, crushing it to bits. Not only will I not be able to contact my team, but Haru won't be able to track me using its embedded GPS device either.

Next it's Starling's turn. The man is rougher as he searches the boy, almost pushing him over at one point. Starling glares up at him but says nothing. It likely would do nothing but make our situation worse.

The man takes anything and everything we might consider using to defend ourselves, or to contact the rest of our team. "Tell me, what do you think your father will say when we tell him you've been helping that chickie over there, and the rest of her team? Do you think he'll overlook it?"

A muscle ticks in Starling's jaw. "My father won't hurt me."

Cold malice glints in the man's eye. "Maybe not, but what do you think he'll do to her?" His eyes travel toward me, making me want to squirm at the disdain that is apparent on his face. "Maybe I'll save him the trouble."

The hairs on the back of my neck stand up as I press myself against the frigid metal partition.

"Don't you dare touch her!" Starling growls, pulling back and delivering a massive punch to the man's jaw.

The suited man recoils, rubbing at his jaw, his expression turning red with fury. "You little shit. If I wasn't under orders I'd kill both of you right now. But I'll have to settle for this." He strides toward me, yanks me up by the arm, and squeezes my thigh over my bandage.

I cry out in agony, trying desperately to withdraw my arm from the man's grasp. But his large hand is clamped on my flesh like a vice-grip. I don't stop fighting. I lunge forward and sink my teeth into his knuckle, drawing hot, metallic blood.

The man howls as he lets go of me, cupping his injured hand in his other meaty fist.

"Stop messing around," Rocket says, sounding more annoyed than anything else. "Chopper, restrain them."

"Yes, sir." He wastes no time pushing past the third man. With practiced movements, he binds our hands and feet with heavy duty zip ties, starting with me. I know different techniques to get out of them, but I can't exactly do anything with three armed Cobalt guys watching me.

Once Starling is bound, he slinks over the floor and leans his shoulder against mine. "Are you all right?" he whispers.

My eyes fall to my bandage, where blood is beginning to seep through from the third man's ruthless grab. "I'm okay." I look over at the scoundrel who hurt me, my resolve set. He's going to regret putting a hand on me. The first chance I get, I'll repay the favor.

Starling leans his head against mine, but his eyes are alert.

I sit up enough to look over at him, noticing that the collar of his peacoat is popped up from the involuntary search.

The corners of my mouth smug smile threatens to splay over my face.

"What is it?" he asks, eyes quizzical.

"Nothing," I mumble, quashing the desire to smirk. But oh, how I want to. Because despite the third man's apparent thoroughness during his searches of Starling and me, the creepy bastard didn't find the tracker I planted on Starling when I hugged him, right after he came down from the attic back at Julep's grandma's house.

Now all we have to do is hope someone on my team finds the signal, before it's too late.

Chapter 20

It doesn't take long for the Cobalt Security team to drive to whatever dark hole they've prepared for us. The armored vehicle lumbers through the streets, seeming to hit every pot hole in the asphalt. I try to force my muscles to relax, but my entire being coils tighter, my teeth clenching each time the car lurches over a divet in the road. My bones start to ache from the rough drive, and I lean against Starling for some semblance of support.

Rocket, Chopper, and the third man sit on the metal bench on the opposite wall, their bodies jostling with each bump. They don't speak, but periodically I catch one of them casting a casual glance at Starling and me. Their prisoners

A cold chill goes through me. I've never been a prisoner before, but that's exactly what we are right now. And if my treatment at the hands of the third man is any indication, it is not going to be a pleasant experience.

I chew the inside of my lip, scanning the interior of the vehicle for anything that might be useful. Aside from the three men and the bench, there's nothing else back here. It's spartan in its lack of any sort of embellishment. And the only cargo is Starling and me. Our gear is unreachable in the floor in front of the passenger seat. I have no doubt that even if I were to get my hands untied and go for my weapon, I'd be shot in the back before I could reach it, leaving Starling alone with mercenaries. Not to mention what another loss would do to the rest of my teammates. Clarity's face, twisted in anguish, is vivid in my mind's eye. Her sobs echo in my ears. No, I have to play this smart. I can't bring more pain on my family if I can avoid it.

Behind my back, I grope with my fingers, despite the limited range of motion, to see if there's a sharp edge I can use to saw through the zip tie that's bound tight around my wrists. No luck.

Inhaling, I try to slow my thoughts. I have to keep my wits about me and stay alive until my family can locate the tracker's signal and catch up to us. Please hurry, guys.

"Hey," Starling whispers into my ear so low that I'm not sure it wasn't merely a breath.

I go still, waiting to hear if he says anything else.

We bounce as the van hits another rough patch in the road, and Starling's knee bounces into mine. After the rocking subsides, he doesn't remove it.

"Hey."

"Yeah?" I whisper in response.

"I'm so sorry about all this. I had no idea—"

"No talking," Rocket barks, shooting an icy look our way.

Starling clamps his mouth shut, and I drop my gaze to my lap. At this point, it's best to pretend to be submissive and attempt not to make the three men mad at us. Experience has taught me that angry men with guns are not to be trifled with, especially when I'm bound and unarmed.

I press my shoulder against Starling's arm, hoping that he understands my meaning. *It's okay. None of this is your fault.* He presses back, lightly, which is reassuring. I take in a deep, calming breath. Whatever happens, we're in this together.

The armored car slows and I perk up, listening for any sounds that might give away our location. Outside, the air is quiet, and then there's the rumble of an engine starting. It doesn't sound like a car, though. It sounds like... I tilt my head up to speak into Starling's ear. He leans down toward my mouth. "We're at the airport, aren't we?" My words are hushed, but the way Starling looks at me when he draws back, with concern on his face, confirms my words. Darnay and his goons are about to transport us somewhere on a private plane. And once we're outside the U.S. we'll be much harder to find and rescue.

My pulse increases. If I could break the bond around my ankles, I might be able to escape from our captors once we're outside the vehicle.

I lock eyes with Starling and mouth, "Ready?"

He gives a slight nod in response, his face drawn in the shadows.

Doubt niggles at my mind. What if Starling doesn't know how to get out of zip ties? Was that something they taught at the academy where he was trained? I huff, frustrated that I don't know this about him.

Rocket shoots a wary look my way, his dark eyes moving over me as if appraising my every limb.

I hunker down and try to look sufficiently cowed, but I don't know if that fools the older man. His eyes narrow, causing my pulse to throb in my throat. The man must be reassured, because after a moment his eyes move away from me toward the windshield.

I bite my lip in frustration. As team leader, it's my job to know each of my teammates' skills so I can delegate tasks accordingly, so why don't I know the extent of Starling's training with bindings? Once we're out of this, all of us are going to need to have a sit down during which we divulge our secret skills. And anyone who doesn't know how to get free from zip ties, duct tape, various knots, and handcuffs is going to get a crash course. It's a crucial skill to know in our line of work. I'm almost amused at the thought of Haru trying to break out of duct tape, but I force the mental image away. This is not the time for daydreaming.

My eyes hone in on the three men between us and the back doors of the vehicle as it moves smoothly over the ground. The pavement here is more well maintained than it was in the city.

All three of the men stand, making sure their weapons are ready. Rocket rolls his shoulders and stretches his neck from side to side. Chopper takes a swig of water from a small canteen hidden in his coat. The third man gives me a grin so disturbing it sends a chill down my spine. At that moment, I decide I'd rather be left alone with Rocket, or Chopper, or Darnay himself than this man. He's 100% certified sinister. My inner alarm bells are going off, sending my adrenaline production into overdrive.

Starling taps his shoulder against mine one more time, and I know he's with me in this, no matter what happens next. I take a deep, steadying breath, and press outward with my feet, testing the tight ring of plastic that's secured around my ankles. The ridges along the band dig into my skin.

"Twister," Rocket says.

My focus snaps to the Cobalt team leader, but he's focused on the third man. His voice is cool and commanding. "Take control of the girl."

So, the devil does have a name. I swallow to push down my nerves. I have to remain alert, on the lookout for a chance to escape from Darnay and his men. Because if we don't, there's no telling what they'll do to us. Or, realistically, to me.

Chapter 21

Twister unlocks and opens the back doors of the vehicle before turning toward us. He steps forward and halls me to my feet. My skin crawls at the sensation of his lumpy fingers wrapped around my arm, but I fight the urge to struggle. There's no point in giving away my intentions while we're still encased in the metal interior of the armored van.

Chopper pulls Starling to his feet, none too gently.

"Let's go," Rocket says, jumping down from the van. "Get them into the plane, quickly."

Chopper and Twister drag us toward the rear of the vehicle, where the doors hang open.

Two more Cobalt Security men in crisp, nondescript black suits appear at the bumper, waiting for us to descend. Their faces are blank of all expression in the light of the moon. If they're surprised that Darnay had their compatriots kidnap two teenagers, they're hiding it well.

I squint through the dark, studying them. Their presence might be an advantage. These men don't know me, and if they're like most of the other people I've encountered as a spy, they'll underestimate a tiny, pixie-haired teenage girl. Let them see how that works out.

Twister yanks me forward and fairly tosses me out of the van toward one of the waiting men. Jostling together, he pulls me away from the car by the arm.

In an instant, I scan the airport grounds until my eyes fix on the plane that's sitting on the apron, engines already rumbling. At first glance, it looks like a luxury plane, but the closer I look, the more I'm certain that it's fortified and probably bulletproof. Its profile is heftier than the average pleasure craft, and several of its rear windows have been covered with metal plating.

Darnay stands at the top of the rollaway steps, watching us with interest. Well, I'm about to give him a show.

With a powerful yell, I jump up, propelling myself off the ground with all of the force I can muster. I swing my legs out and up before dragging them back toward the ground, pulling my ankles apart with all my might. The zip tie breaks with a satisfying snap, and my legs are free. Twisting out of the man's grip on my arm, I twirl around, sending a well-aimed kick to his groin. His eyes widen in shock as he doubles over in pain.

I jump again, tucking my legs against my chest so I can pull my arms under my feet and into my stomach. My arms whip out, reaching for the gun in the holster at his waist. The tips of my fingers graze the soft leather of the clasp. I've almost got it.

Pop.

The high-pitched sound cuts through the air above the noise of the plane's engine, and my eyes go wide. I know that sound. Even if I could reach with my hands still bound, there isn't time to evade the spines of the taser that's just been fired. It's too late. The pins cling to the back of my shirt, burrowing into the fabric and pinching my flesh. My muscles start to seize, and I scream as my body falls to the ground. My cheek slams against the asphalt and tiny pebbles dig into my skin. The pain stops, and rough hands pull me off the ground.

"Loveday!" Starling's voice is laced with panic.

I gasp for air, thankful that the pain is over, but I freeze when I meet the eyes of the man whose hands are gripping my arms. Twister looks down at me, his cool expression more frightening even than his calculating grin.

I try to recoil away from him, but his grip on my arms tightens, making me wince in pain as he squeezes my skin. "Try something like that again, and I'll shoot you myself."

I gulp at the current of eagerness in his tone.

"Leave her alone," Starling says, his voice cracking.

The man merely rolls his eyes before throwing me over his shoulder and carrying me to the plane like an uncooperative toddler. His hard shoulder digs into my ribs as he stomps up the stairs, but I bite down any sounds of indignation. Letting on how uncomfortable my position is won't do me any good.

Lifting my head, I scan the area around the airport. There's no movement, no light, nothing. Any hope that my teammates have found the tracker's signal is dwindling. My team only has minutes to arrive before we're in the air, flying to who knows where.

Come on, guys, I breathe, willing my teammates to appear on the other side of the chain link fence surrounding the airport property.

A few yards behind, Chopper is escorting Starling after us. Starling's eyes lock on mine. "Are you okay?" he mouths. I give a slight head shake, not daring to do more in case it angers the pack animal who is hauling me toward the plane as if I'm no heavier than a normal carry-on.

My gaze falls on the trees that line the perimeter fence. They're dark and silent under the moon's pale glow, their leaves heavy in the still night air.

There's a flicker of light between two trunks, but then it goes out. I squint, not sure I actually saw anything. I stare at the same spot, but there's nothing. It must have been wishful thinking, or a lightning bug.

Wait. There it is again.

Starling catches the direction of my gaze but doesn't attempt to look behind him. Smart guy.

Relief bubbles up in my chest, but I suppress it to maintain the element of surprise. If my teammates are going to spring Starling and I from our captors' clutches, they'll need all of the advantages they can get. My features remain stoic, but inside I'm beaming. That's my team. It has to be. And they're here right on time.

Twister grunts as he stomps up the stairs, still carrying me over his shoulder.

Darnay steps aside so we can enter the plane, sneering at me as Twister passes into the interior of the craft.

"Hello, again, Loveday. That was an interesting trick you pulled, breaking the bond around your legs. You'll have to teach me how to do it sometime."

I glare at him, not deigning to respond. His patronizing tone makes me want to vomit all over his fancy, cream-colored button up and pristine ivory slacks. Maybe I could even ruin his patent leather loafers.

Twister throws me into one of the immaculate, black leather seats and handcuffs my still-bound wrists to one of the armrests.

Chopper drags Starling in next, handcuffing him to the seat next to me. He's straightening up again when gunfire fills the air.

"They're here!" I yell in excitement and relief. My eyes find

113

Starling's and I'm actually smiling. The corner of his mouth turns up in response.

Chopper and Twister lunge for the door, peeking out of the opening with guns drawn. Rocket stands at their back, his fingers wrapped around his own weapon.

There's a break in the gunfire, and the Cobalt Security guys shoot back.

I close my eyes, listening for cries of pain from my teammates, but hear nothing under the shots being fired.

"Get us out of here," Darnay calls to the pilot. Then he flings himself into a chair. His seat belt clicks into place over his lap.

The pilot nods, his hands gripping the wheel.

"Shut the damn door. We're leaving. Now!"

"The rest of my men are still out there," Rocket says, gesturing toward the hatch, even as the plane begins to creep forward.

"Leave them."

Rocket sets his jaw. "Yes, sir."

Twister and Chopper step back from the opening, and Rocket closes the door with a slam, rotating the lock into place.

The aircraft picks up speed as outside, bullets ricochet off the fuselage. The rumble of the engines increases. Painted runway lines begin to blur outside the window. The front wheels leave the ground.

The gunfire ceases as the whine of the plane's engines rises, filling my ears.

The back wheels leave the ground, and we're airborne.

Rocket, Chopper, and Twister settle into seats near the front of the plane, their expressions not betraying any frustration they might be feeling at having left an untold number of their crew behind.

Silence stretches out as we hurdle higher into the air, the sky beyond the windows a screen of white clouds. My ears ring with the sound of phantom gunfire. I clamp my eyes closed, willing the sting at the back of my eyes to subside. Starling and I might be captives right now, but our team won't give up on us. They'll find us, somehow.

Starling leans toward me in his seat, bumping me with his shoulder. "They'll come for us."

"I know." But how long will it take, and what will Darnay do to us in the meantime?

As if summoned by my thoughts, Darnay gets out of his seat and strides toward us, frowning. "What a futile rescue attempt that was."

My fuse is lit, but I can't do much handcuffed to a chair. I wait until Darnay is within striking distance, and fling my foot toward his kneecap.

He jumps out of the way easily. "Uh uh. That's not very nice." He wags a finger at me, clearly enjoying having the upper hand.

A string of colorful curses filters through my mind, but I bite my tongue.

Darnay smirks as his attention swings from me to Starling.

I look over at the boy beside me and am surprised to see the wide, fearful expression on his face. Starling is legitimately afraid of his own father. What kind of monster is this man?

If Darnay notices his son's pale visage, he doesn't acknowledge it. Instead, he stands casually with his hands on his hips. "Now, son, I'd very much like to talk about how disappointed I was to learn that you were still working with Royal's team, despite the fact that he alone is responsible for the death of your mother. And I thought family meant so much to you. I guess I was wrong."

His words are cool and calculating, much more elegant than a simple sucker punch to the gut. But they hit their mark.

Starling withdraws as if he's been struck, and his gaze falls to the ground. His mouth clamps shut.

I glare at Darnay, but he doesn't acknowledge it. Despite our precarious position, assurance rises in my chest. Darnay is wrong. Family means everything to Starling. Clarity, Lotus, Julep, Haru, and me, we're his family now. Not Charles Darnay, a man who missed much of Starling's childhood, and who now is trying to destroy the family we've built.

"I'm sorry, Father."

"You should be. It's going to take some work to make this up to me." Darnay's gaze flicks toward me. "We'll have to figure something out."

"I won't harm Loveday, so don't even consider asking."

When I look at Starling again, his mouth has taken on a hard edge. Resolve seeps into the corners of his eyes. Whatever fear he feels regarding his father, he's fighting it.

"We'll see." Darnay's cool tone makes my blood chill. Despite his calm exterior, I know what Darnay did to that analyst back in D.C. And if he wanted to make Royal suffer, a quick and simple way to do that would be to cut off my hands or feet or tongue, have them gift wrapped, and send the package to my father. Fear blooms in my chest, like flames licking at dry paper, and I press my lips together as my mouth goes dry.

Chapter 22

"Even the closest allies can be turned, given the right application of leverage."

Royal's words filter through my head as I look at Starling. What sort of training did he receive in resisting interrogation techniques? And how effective will that training be against the man who gave him life and who knows exactly which pressure points to trigger to get the reaction he wants?

I gulp. This is where I have to exercise trust, even when my training is screaming at me that everyone breaks eventually. Once Starling breaks, what happens then?

My eyes roll up toward the ceiling as I press my head into the seat at my back. The cabin is dark but for narrow lights that run the length of the plane, just above the windows. Darnay's even breathing indicates that he's asleep, but his goons are still alert. Rocket glances toward us then away again, his face blank.

I chew on the inside of my lip. I don't have any experience with being interrogated, aside from the admittedly slight training Royal gave us on resisting interrogation techniques, but I know he was probably right. Everyone breaks eventually. Even me.

Further, I might be especially vulnerable because of my emotional ties to each of my teammates. If I have a choice, I won't hurt any of them, and that makes me weak. It's a liability Royal saw far before this moment, even though the truth of it is just now trickling down my spine, like the chilling drip of rain on my bare skin.

I glance over at Starling, appraising him. How long will I resist before giving up information that compromises him? How long before I betray Lotus or Julep? Before I serve up my sister on a silver platter?

I inhale, running through everything Royal told me about resistance. My name is Loveday. My rank is Team Leader. I repeat these two phrases in my head. They're the only information I'm allowed to disclose, that is, until I break.

Starling shifts in his seat, his brown eyes staring out the window without registering the stars that twinkle off the plane's wing. We've been over the ocean for hours. I have no idea where we are now.

What sort of information will Darnay require of me? What will he ask for, in exchange for a reprieve from his hold? Reality comes crashing in. There isn't much that I know that would be of use to Darnay, not now that he has taken over control of the Tower. Even now, I imagine he has computer techs there, hacking through our security systems and gaining access to whatever files are partitioned on the computers in the control room. Royal shielded me and my teammates from so much of the classified information for this very reason: so that we'd be useless in an interrogation setting. Usually, that would mean we would be safe, but in my current situation I'm anything but.

And once Royal retires, I'll be the point woman for any and all jobs we take, either from the CIA or from businesses in the private sector. I'll have my finger in every pie, which means I'll be a valuable resource if I'm ever captured again. I ball my fists, vowing to myself. After this job, I'm never going to be captured again. I can't roll over on my teammates if I'm not captured. I won't do it. Because they don't make me weak; they make me strong. They give me a whole slew of people to fight for, even when it appears the battle has already been lost.

I glance at Starling again, and he meets my eyes. He's one more person in my corner. He's someone worth fighting for, no matter how bleak our situation.

Darnay stirs, sitting up in his seat and twisting to look at us. His lips flatten, and then he's pushing to a stand. "Now, Loveday," he says, coming to stand before me, his limbs balancing effortlessly despite the plane's movement. "Let's have a little chat, shall we?" He sits in the chair across the aisle from mine and turns his body toward me. "Have you figured out where we're going?"

I school my features until my expression gives away nothing, then I meet Darnay's almost amused look with a blank stare.

"No? I'll tell you. We're going to the Philippines. My wife was from there. Did you know that?" He clucks his tongue. "No? Well, she was. I met her during a mission, and fell in love the moment I saw her. She was stunning, intelligent. She knew how to make me laugh." His eyes turn cold. "No one makes me laugh anymore. Do you know why I'm telling you this?"

I don't respond. Let him spin his tale of love and tragic loss. Inwardly, I can admit that it was a horrible thing, the way his wife died. But that doesn't justify Darnay's relentless pursuit of revenge over the past two decades. The innocent lives he's taken.

"Can't guess? I'll tell you. Maureen was the breath of life itself, and your father killed her in cold blood and didn't feel even a hint of remorse. My best friend *killed* my wife. Can you imagine such a thing? Unfortunately for him, Royal was never cold-blooded enough to truly succeed in this business. You see, to be a good spy, you have to detach from your emotions. You can't let the relationships that social mores dictate are important get in the way of your goals. Royal made that mistake: getting married, having a child. And then when his wife died, he quit. Didn't have the stomach for our work anymore. But I did. You see, I can play at being a bumbling hotel owner with a strained relationship with my son, but none of that is real. The only thing real will be the triumph I feel as I watch Royal's life leave his eyes. Then you'll see how meaningless relationships are, because they never last."

As Darnay talks, Starling grows painfully still beside me, his frown deepening. Once Darnay is done spouting his drivel, the interior of the plane grows quiet. The seconds tick by as I wait. It's an interrogation tactic, I know—keeping silent to force the other person to speak to break the awkwardness.

"How can you say relationships are meaningless?" Starling asks, meeting his father's eyes with an injured look of his own. "If relationships meant nothing to you, why have you spent so many years seeking revenge for Mum's death? It doesn't make sense. You're contradicting yourself."

Darnay studies his son for a moment, head tilted to one side. "That is where you're wrong. Maureen's life brought meaning to mine. She was the answer to everything. Only in her death did she render relationships meaningless."

"But Father, what about me? You could have had a close relationship with me, but instead you..."

"Pushed you away? Yes, well. That is what happens when your son looks so much like his mother. It's remarkable, really, how much you favor her. Then, as you grew, it became apparent to me that you were too focused on finding meaningful ties to the people around you to be useful. You were too in touch with messy emotions. And now I discover you're so besotted with Royal's daughter that you'd betray your own father."

Color creeps up Starling's neck.

"Don't pretend to be surprised, Armando. Your feelings for Loveday, here, are as obvious as the sky is blue. Really, if you're going to work as a spy you ought to learn to hide your emotions better. It makes you such an easy target. For example, if were to, say, break each of her fingers one by one, what might you do?"

Starling lunges from his seat, free hand outstretched and nostrils flaring, but is yanked back violently by the handcuff anchoring him to the chair.

The movement is so sudden I jump, caught completely off guard.

"See? Predictable." Darnay sneers. "Lucky for you, I already have the information I need." His eyes flick over me. "Get some sleep, dear. We'll be in Manila in less than a day, and then you'll be required to say goodbye to your dear old dad. An eye for an eye, you know." He winks at me before standing, dusting invisible lint off his pants before returning to his own seat.

I turn to Starling. "Are you all right?" I whisper.

He shakes his head slightly, eyes downturned. "I can't believe he's being so vile. My own father." His eyes slide closed. "Hearing him threaten to hurt you like that... I couldn't bear it. I wanted to... to..."

Warmth builds in my chest. "Shh, I know. But we have to hold it together. You can't let him see that he's bothering you, or he'll use it against you. He was just trying to find your pressure points. We're going to be fine, okay?" I swallow, hoping my words sound more reassuring than I feel. Truthfully, I want to sit on my hands to hide my still-intact fingers from Darnay's view so he doesn't get any ideas.

Starling inhales through his nose, and nods. "All right."

"Good."

Inside, I'm fuming. Anger at Darnay's nauseating condescension is making my stomach turn. I look out the window to the pitch-black beyond, willing time to slow down.

Because if Darnay has his way in the Philippines, my father will be gone forever. And if I have my way, Starling will have to say goodbye to his father, although admittedly, that is no great loss. Either way, we both suffer.

Chapter 23

I strain against the handcuff on my wrist to see out the window, but the metal bites into my skin, making me sit back in my seat. No matter how hard I pull, I can't see even a glimpse of the archipelagos that make up the Philippines. From the front of the plane, I heard one of the men speaking to Darnay in a low voice, letting him know that we'll be landing in an hour. So I know the small Asian country is just out the window, if only I could get a glimpse of it.

The flight was an interminably long seventeen hours, with only one bathroom break. And even fewer snack breaks. If Darnay's goal was to make me uncomfortable and on edge, he's got me right where he wants me. Not even Starling could convince him to give us something to eat. My stomach growls angrily and I glare at the back of Darnay's seat. The more time I spend with the guy, the less I like him. Not that I ever liked him in the first place. There may have been a grudging respect, but even that little bit of charity was dashed by his single-minded focus on revenge. He's done nothing but pace back and forth for most of the flight, eyes gleaming with sinister intent. And when he wasn't pacing, he was in his seat, poring over satellite images of something I couldn't quite make out.

An area with patches of green and gray. A park, maybe.

The plane shudders before beginning its descent. I watch out the window as the sky goes from blue to white to blue again. I've lost all sense of time, but from the shade of the skyline, I can tell it's late afternoon in the Philippines. Halloween.

"Did you get any sleep?" Starling asks, voice low.

I shake my head, feeling both exhausted and wired, on top of famished. In less than 24 hours, this will all be over, one way or the other.

"Me neither."

I glance over at the boy beside me, noting the red rim around his eyes, the way his hair lays flat and uncombed over his head. His clothing is rumpled and musty.

I probably don't look much better. I can feel the bags under my eyes, and my head feels like it weighs fifty pounds, which is much more than my neck can support. I wish I could simply close my eyes and sleep, but I can't. I don't trust Darnay and his goons not to do something awful while I'm out, like toss me out of the plane into the ocean or something. I'd be one less loose end to tie up.

As if he can read my thoughts, Twister turns in his chair and eyes me, one corner of his mouth curling up in a wicked smirk.

My hackles rise. I'd like to wipe that stupid, predatory look right off his face, but instead I force the thoughts down. Push my facial muscles into a calm expression. Provoking Twister now won't do either of us any good, and it'll only make it more fun for him.

The plane glides toward the ground, its wheels skimming through the air and touching down on the runway with effortless ease.

The Cobalt Security guys stand, checking to make sure their gear is in order. Rocket bends low to listen to something Darnay is saying, both of them glancing in our direction.

My pulse quickens. Here we go. I take a deep, steadying breath without taking my eyes off them.

Starling reaches over and rests his free hand on my knee, not taking his own gaze from his father. It's a clear message that his allegiance is with me and not Darnay.

I hold my chin higher, waiting for the reaction that I'm sure is coming. But nothing happens.

Darnay barely registers Starling's gesture before turning his focus to the hushed conversation he's having with Rocket.

Starling tenses beside me but doesn't withdraw his hand.

The casual way Darnay ignores his son makes me want to scream at him. How dare he care so little about his only child, his own flesh and blood? How dare he put a twenty-year-old vendetta before his relationship with Starling? But it's clear that he does, and that he always has. I won't make the same mistake.

I put my free hand over Starling's, curling my pale fingers around his longer brown ones. I lean toward the boy who has sneaked into my heart and stolen it, almost without my noticing. Licking my lips, I speak. "Whatever happens, I'm glad you're with me."

Our eyes lock, and I hope he can see in my gaze just how glad I am. How thankful I am that Royal brought him onto our team, even when I fought it tooth and nail. Even when I pushed him away with every fiber of my being.

He must see something in my face, because the corners of Starling's mouth twitch upward ever so slightly, and then he's leaning toward me.

My eyes slip closed as his nose brushes against mine.

125

"Time to go, chickie."

My eyes fly open at the closeness of Twister's gruff words, and I press back against my chair.

The man is standing over me, reaching toward my bound wrist with a tiny handcuff key. Unlocking it with a deft hand, he pulls me out of my seat and shoves me toward the plane door.

"Where are you taking her?" Starling asks, a forced calm in rippling under the words.

"Relax. You're coming too," Rocket says, waving Chopper toward where Starling is seated.

In a minute, we're both being marched over the concrete in the direction of a white SUV.

Around us, there's almost no one at the airport. There's a line of planes near the terminal but no ground crew or workers driving carts carrying baggage. It's quiet, the only sounds our footfalls as we approach the vehicle.

I look upward, taking in the pink and orange streaks across the sky as they recede toward the horizon, where the sun is setting behind the dark water of the South China Sea. The warmth in the air surprises me. It's thick and humid compared to the crisp temperatures we left behind in D.C.

Twister opens the back door of the SUV and folds the seat forward before shoving me into the back row. I scramble across the bench seat as Starling climbs in beside me. The car door shuts with a slam, and then Darnay and the three Cobalt men get into vehicle, Chopper on Starling's other side, Twister in the middle seat with Darnay, and Rocket up front with the driver.

I keep my eyes focused ahead so I can keep all of the car's passengers in sight, as well as watch where we're going. The more I'm able to orient myself, the better off we'll be if we manage to escape from the people holding us captive.

We drive through wide paved streets filled with vehicles of all kinds. Several motorcycles zip past us and up the street. Beside the SUV, a tiny doorless cart packed to the brim with people weaves in and out of traffic like a drunken man liable to keel over at any moment. I take in a breath as the car squeezes between two larger sedans, just fitting in the space, before disappearing into the traffic up ahead.

The road is lined with grubby concrete and brick buildings. Aging billboards are mounted in the spaces between streaked windows. A tarp is draped over a storefront, and underneath colorful dresses hang from a sagging clothesline. Another motorcycle flies past, drawing my attention to the road ahead.

We pull off the wide road onto a narrower one, passing darkened concrete buildings zig zagged with power lines. Up ahead, there's a green space dotted with trees that loom larger in the waning light.

The SUV draws even with it, and my eyes widen in surprise. It's a cemetery, but unlike the streets and buildings around it, the burial ground looks immaculate. All of the grass has been evenly cut, the trees and shrubs are meticulously shaped, and there's not a piece of trash to be seen. Tall lamps are lit throughout the green space, throwing swaths of light over the graves.

Our driver makes an abrupt left and pulls into an underground parking garage.

Darnay and his men disembark from the car before pulling Starling and I out of the back seat. They tie our hands behind our backs and walk us up a poorly lit stairwell to a shabbily decorated apartment on the third floor. There's no one in sight along the hall as Darnay takes a tarnished key from his pocket and unlocks the door. A single light bulb flickers to life overhead. It's a simple domed-glass fixture with a brass knob in the center. The air in the room is stale and unmoving, as if it's been vacated for quite some time, and I can't stop the cough that scrapes my dry throat as Chopper marches me inside.

Rocket gestures toward a dingy brown couch that faces the large, unadorned window. "Have a seat."

I give a slow nod before shuffling across the room and sinking onto the sofa, allowing my head to rest against the cushions. I'm probably going to get eaten by the dust bunnies living in this thing, but I'm too wrung out to care. My head lols to the side as I take in my surroundings. To my left, there's an ancient television set covered in years of dust, sitting on a wooden cabinet. Above it, along the wall, there are photographs in frames that were once shiny silver but are now gray-green with years of grime and neglect. A chill runs down my spine. Where are we, exactly? This is not the sort of place I associate with Darnay. There is no cold, shiny marble or immaculate, velvety leather furniture here.

Starling moves to stand facing me, his back against the window. Even with his hands tied behind his back, he watches the men take up positions. His expression is stoic, like a true silent sentinel.

Darnay disappears into what I assume is the bedroom, not even glancing in our direction.

"Starling?" Darnay calls from the other room. "Come here a minute. We need to talk." His voice sounds loose and cracked, like he's forgotten the careful modulation he usually employs.

Starling's eyes flit toward mine before he marches out of the room.

I swivel around on the couch to stare at the doorway he's just vacated, wondering what Darnay could possibly have to say to his son after everything that has happened.

The silence in the apartment grows as Rocket shifts on his feet near the door.

Chopper sits on a tall stool overlooking the kitchen counter, and Twister takes up position outside the bedroom door, barring anyone from getting in or out. His dark eyes slide over to me, his expression blank. It's even more unsettling than when he smiles.

Even though my hands are tied behind my back, I manage to push to a stand and limp over to the window to look out into the night. The road is dark between the rings made by the streetlights. Across the way is the cemetery we passed. It's darker now and much harder to see, but I can't tear my eyes away from the playground in the corner, its perimeter a circle of park benches. In the center, there's a line of swings, and an old slide, its paint peeling away from the metal surface.

My heart is in my throat as I whirl around, taking in the outdated decor and furniture, the photographs that haven't been touched in decades. The insect carcases that dot the carpet. My eyes land on the cluster of frames where they hang crooked on the wall, and in my gut, I know where we are. Striding as quickly as I can over to the wall, I stare up at it, wishing I could wipe away the grit so I could get a better look at the faces behind the glass.

Pulling at the bindings on my hands, I twist my wrists back and forth in an effort to loosen them. It doesn't work. There is no freeing my hands. A grunt of frustration rumbles in my throat.

"Want a better look?" Twister asks with a smirk. He lifts his chin toward Chopper, who picks his way toward me, careful not to step on any of the dead bugs. His hand doesn't leave his weapon. Reaching over me, the man takes the frame off the wall and, after peering at how filthy the glass is, he wipes the smudged surface on the front of my shirt.

I bite back the disgusted noise that rises to my lips, and stare down at the wide swirl of dust on the black fabric.

"Here, take a look." He holds the photo up to my face, but far enough away that he could snatch it back in a blink.

I shiver as I look at the image: a pretty Filipino woman holding a smiling one year old in her arms, both of them crowned with shiny black hair over fawn brown skin. Their deep brown eyes are lit with happiness, because they don't yet know how their story ends. But I do.

Chapter 24

Several minutes pass before Starling emerges from the bedroom, his face pale. He walks over to me with his eyes downturned and his jaw set. In a move that appears without contemplation, he sinks onto the couch beside me and slumps back against the cushions.

I lean toward him and tap my shoulder against his arm. "Are you okay?" I whisper.

He doesn't respond, not right away. His eyes close and his adam's apple bobs.

"Starling?"

The boy's eyes slide open, and his lips part. "I…"

"Loveday, have you figured out where we are yet?" Darnay saunters around the couch to stand over me, a conniving smile on his smug face.

I lift my chin and set my face in what I hope is a defiant expression.

"No?" He clucks his tongue. "I expected more from you. Royal's star student." He rolls his eyes as he says this, and then lifts his hand to study his pristine fingernails. "I'm surprised you don't know where we are."

"This is your wife's family's apartment. I'm guessing her

parents from the photos of her and young Starling, and the lack of pictures of you. Not a fan of you, were they?" I slide my foot toward Starling's and press gently, hoping to convey that I'm not trying to hurt him. I'm merely trying to remind Darnay that I'm not to be trifled with, even when my hands are bound.

Darnay smirks. "There's the mouthy know-it-all I've come to know and... Well, nevermind. Can you guess why I brought you here, specifically? No? I'll tell you. I thought it would be nice for Starling to see where his mother grew up. He always wanted to see it, as a child, although I never got around to bringing him here. But now, now that I'm so close to catching Maureen's killer, it seemed a fitting time to visit. Don't you think?"

"Don't give me that sentimental crap. The only reason you're here is because you think manipulating your son emotionally will get him on your side, you selfish ass. Nevermind the fact that you've killed countless innocents over the past twenty years, sacrificial lambs for your blood lust."

For just a moment, Darnay's expression slips and I see the fury smouldering behind his eyes. Then the mask is firmly in place. "Such strong opinions for one so young. Someday, you will see that the world isn't so black and white. There are no good guys and bad guys; there are only people, and we're all shades of gray. My son," he pauses, adding weight to the word, "understands this, which is why he's going to call Royal and deliver a message for me."

Starling's eyes fly to his father's face.

"What message?" I ask, eyes narrowed.

"Simply that if Royal doesn't show up at Holy Trinity Memorial Park tomorrow, at 19:00, he'll kill you. Sounds fair, don't you think?"

"He would never harm me."

Darnay's mouth curves upward into a Grinchy grin.

I keep my expression confident, even though a flutter of nerves is working its way from my fingertips toward my chest.

"Are you so sure about that?" Darnay says, taking out a phone and dialing. He holds it up to Starling's ear. "You know what to say."

I can just hear Royal answering on the other end. "Charles? Are you there?"

"Speak," Darnay mouths to his son, and with a glance at my stricken face, Starling does.

My stew sits half eaten and congealed in my lap. The bites I managed to get down my throat leap and twirl in my stomach, forcing me to clamp my eyes shut and take deep, controlled breaths to push the bile down. No matter what happens tomorrow at 19:00, I know Starling won't hurt me. I *know* it. And yet, hearing him say those words to my dad made my stomach revolt against digesting the meager meal provided for us by Chopper, who was sent down the street to retrieve it.

Since the phone call, Darnay hasn't left Starling and I alone at all. He's given us no time to touch base with each other, so although we're sitting mere inches apart on the old couch, it feels as if we're not even in the same hemisphere. If he's hoping to put a wedge between us, the awkward silence is a definite start.

The man stands at the window, peering down at the cemetery below, his arms relaxed at his sides in the silence of the apartment.

Cars drive along the street, their way illuminated by headlights that catch my eyes and make me wonder each time if it's my teammates, come at last to free me from Darnay and his lackeys. But each time the car continues down the road without pausing, as if this whole apartment building has been forgotten, its occupants long gone.

I know they found the tracker I planted on Starling's coat, because how else would they have followed us to the airport? Unless... Haru found Darnay's flight plan some via other means. It wouldn't surprise me. She's astonishingly adept at thwarting cyber-security measures and accessing information that she shouldn't be able to find. And if it's true that they didn't actually find the tracker's signal, then there's no way for them to know where we are. No way for my team to rescue us before Darnay's deadline. No way to end this crusade for revenge before tomorrow at 19:00. And I'd really rather we end this before then, because I do not want to watch Royal march out to that bench unarmed and face Darnay. But if nothing changes in the next few hours, that's exactly what I'll have to do, and I'm terrified of what will happen after that.

Darnay's sudden turn from the window almost makes me jump. A corner of his mouth lifts at my reaction as he walks toward the bedroom. "Rocket, take the first shift. Chopper and Twister, get some sleep. We'll switch in four hours."

"Yes, sir," all three men respond.

Chopper and Twister produce rolled mats from the closet by the front door, spread them out on the floor, and lay down. They're asleep in a minute, as if there's a button they can press to go to sleep on command.

Rocket moves to the door and stands against it, arms folded in front of him, eyes clear and focused.

Starling and I are finally sort of alone.

My body relaxes in relief. I shift so I can get a better look at him, but my lips feel glued together. What do I even say to him? Words and phrases float through my mind, but nothing seems sufficient. So instead I yawn widely and lay my head back against the cushions.

"Hey," he whispers, nudging my knee with his own.

My eyes flutter toward his even as they droop closed. I'm so exhausted at this point I can barely keep them open.

"You know I would never hurt you, right? No matter what happens tomorrow," he swallows, "you can count on me. I'm on your side, always."

I'll never admit it to him, but my insides uncoil at his assurance. Then guilt washes through me. I should trust him by now. I should, but my years of espionage work, not to mention Royal's penchant for withholding information, have made me a suspicious cynic. But Starling doesn't deserve distrust. He's done everything but swear a blood oath in fealty to me. "I know."

"We'll get out of this, somehow, and we'll save your dad. We won't let my... er... Darnay hurt him. No more losses, remember?"

I nod, remembering the promise I made my team, but the problem is, if we succeed, if we stop Darnay from killing my father, Starling will lose his father. Darnay will end up in prison, probably for the rest of his life. And that's the best case scenario. Worst case? Lethal injection. And that's not counting the other countries that will want a piece of him once the U.S. lets its allies know that Charles Darnay is the wanted criminal Nexus.

"Do you remember this place, at all?"

Starling shakes his head. "I haven't been back here since she died." He turns away from me to study the frames on the wall.

I wish Chopper would wipe them off so we could see their faces, but I doubt my shirt could take it. My eyes focus on the single visible photo: the one of baby Starling in his mother's arms.

"You do look a lot like her," I whisper. "Thank goodness."

He's somber as he turns to face me, sending a furtive glance toward the bedroom door. "Sometimes I wonder what else I got from her. Was she friendly and eager, like me, or am I—"

"You're nothing like him." My words are sure, and I can tell by the way Starling's entire form eases that it's exactly what he was worried about.

Pulling his legs up onto the couch, he sinks down against its arm. "Come here. We should try to get some rest."

I cast my eyes toward Rocket, Chopper, and Twister, who haven't moved. Twister's faint snoring filters through the air. I'm not sure falling asleep is a good idea, given that it would leave us vulnerable to Darnay's goons.

"They won't hurt us," Starling says. He's so sure of it that I don't bother to argue. Instead, I lean in to the wariness that's wrapped around my spine, choosing to trust Starling's instincts in this moment.

I recline back against him, letting him sandwich my legs with his own. Once I'm situated with my head resting against his shoulder, he tucks his arms around me and rests his head against the tall arm of the couch. "Get some sleep," he whispers, and his breath fans the hair on top of my head. "We'll worry about tomorrow… tomorrow."

I've never fallen asleep in a man's arms, his heartbeat a steady rhythm against my back, his warmth surrounding me. It's so warm and soothing I can almost forget that we're prisoners of a ruthless, revenge-hungry super spy. Inhaling deeply, I regulate my breathing, close my eyes… and welcome sleep.

Chapter 25

A looming presence moves into my awareness, ushering me toward wakefulness. The back of my neck prickles, and my eyes pop open. I roll out of Starling's relaxed arms and onto the ground, crouching with my fingers brushing the carpet, eyes alert.

Chopper stands behind the couch holding a large white paper bag. Garlic and other scents I can't place linger in the air. My stomach voices its hunger, which makes the corners of Chopper's mouth twitch. "Hungry? I brought you and lover-boy breakfast."

From his post near the apartment door, Twister rolls his eyes. Apparently it's Rocket's turn on the cot.

"Huh?" Starling yawns awake, sitting up and stretching his arms over his head. A narrow groan escapes his lips, and then his nostrils flare. "What is that? It smells delicious." His eyes fall on me, on my coiled stance, and it's as if he remembers where he is. His eyebrows fly upward as he pivots to face Chopper. "What's going on?"

Chopper shrugs. "Nothing. I was ordered to get you two some breakfast." He thrusts the paper bag into Starling's chest and saunters to the back of the apartment carrying another takeout container.

My muscles relax as the soldier retreats away from us, and I push to stand. "What is it?"

The white paper rustles as Starling unfolds the top and peers inside. "It looks like… fried rice and eggs? Are you hungry?"

I send a furtive glance toward where Twister is standing, his body stiff and gaze alert. It doesn't look like he's going to bother us while we eat, so I sink down onto the couch beside Starling. "I could eat."

We chew the salty, garlicky rice and runny fried eggs quietly, the only sounds in the apartment the scraping of plastic forks on styrofoam. Near the door, Twister and Chopper are eating their breakfast as well, and I assume Darnay is doing the same in the bedroom. He has yet to make an appearance this morning, but even so his presence hangs over us like a stormcloud heavy with rain yet to be spilled.

Outside, the sky is beginning to transform from cool blue to the warmer pinks and oranges of morning. Already, some early risers are mulling about the cemetery setting up tents near grave sites or sales booths along the sidewalk. I scan the area but don't see any traces of my teammates. I'm more than a little worried about why they didn't attempt to breach the apartment during the night.

"Where are they?" I murmur, still watching the movement on the sidewalk below.

"Who?" Starling whispers, looking up from his breakfast to meet my eyes.

"You know, our team."

"I'm sure they're nearby."

I bite the inside of my cheek. "Why didn't they come during the night?"

"Perhaps it took them time to arrange a flight here from Atlanta. They'll be here soon."

"Yeah. You're right. They're probably somewhere out of sight, strategizing right now." I hope.

"Indeed."

We fall back into a silence that would be comfortable if it weren't for the men with guns standing mere yards away from us.

The last drops of water slide down the interior of the paper cup and drop onto my tongue. I crumple the vessel and stuff it into the paper bag with the rest of the debris, all that remains of our breakfast. Standing, I march over to where all three of Darnay's goons are standing near the door. "I need to use the bathroom."

"Good morning, Loveday." Darnay rambles out of the bedroom toward me. "Had a good breakfast, I assume?"

I scowl at him, not dignifying his smug face with a response.

"Good, good." He reaches out to pat my shoulder, but I step back out of his reach. Darnay clucks his tongue. "Is that any way to treat an old friend of your father's?" His lips curl upward as if the words are as distasteful to him as they are to me.

"I'd hardly call a narcissistic murderer an old friend of my dad's."

Darnay's reaction is lightning fast: a closed fist to my open mouth.

My head snaps back as my teeth dig into my lip, splitting it open. Blood oozes down my chin. I touch my throbbing mouth with shaking fingers, which come away with crimson tips. My tongue runs over my teeth, but thankfully none of them feel chipped or loose.

"Father!" Starling is off the couch in a flash, running over to place himself between Darnay and me. "Don't you touch her again."

Darnay rolls his eyes. "Maybe this will teach her some respect. Or at least some restraint." He rubs casually at his knuckles as he speaks.

Starling makes a disgusted sound and turns his back on his father, turns toward me. "Are you all right?"

The pulsing pain is beginning to lessen, so I nod. "I think so."

"Let's get you into the bathroom and wash up, shall we?" He puts an arm around me and ushers me in the direction of the hallway.

"There's something I want you to do first," Darnay says, stepping in front of us. "There's a phone call I'd like you to make." Despite the cavalier tone of his voice, the hard edge in his eyes made it clear that this wasn't a request.

Folding up the hem of my shirt, I wipe at my chin. "Fine."

Darnay retrieves a phone from the pocket of his slacks and hands it to me. "Make a video call to your father. Remind him of our meeting. Let him see your bloody mouth. That should be enough to bring him here."

My face twists in revulsion. "You're despicable."

Darney's eyes flash with anger. "Don't make me hit you again, Loveday."

"Don't try to blame it on her, you coward."

The man's expression turns to ice as he swivels toward his son. "You'll see soon enough that I am no coward."

The two of them are squared off against each other, the fury sparking between them. Darnay's control is slipping, and I don't want to see what will happen if he loses it completely.

"Hey, he's not worth it." I pull on Starling's arm, forcing him to look at me. "Let it go."

Slowly, the anger seeps out of his expression, and he gives me a small nod.

"Thanks," I whisper, gripping his hand. Then I turn to face Darnay with all the vehemence I can muster. "Where in the park do you want him to meet you?"

Darnay's eyes are flint pebbles as he looks at me. "He'll know the place when he sees it." He turns away from me, but pauses. Over his shoulder, he says, "Make it quick."

Running my tongue over my teeth one more time to check that they're secure, I walk over to the window and scan the cemetery and park. There are more people now, parking cars, leaving bouquets propped against headstones, and lighting candles.

Starling hovers beside me, casting frequent glances toward my bloodied mouth.

Why would Darnay want Royal to meet him in the park, of all places? All I can see are undulations of crisply cut grass, gravestones, flowers, well-manicured shrubs and trees. A glint of the sun shines off something metallic on the far side of the park: the worn metal slide, with a ladder leading to the top.

Chapter 26

The vision of my busted-up face has Darnay's desired effect. Royal goes stiff as soon as he sees me. His jaw forms a hard line and his eyes burn hot. "What have they done to you?" His words are low and rough and pulsing with anger. I don't think I've ever seen him livid like this.

"It's not as bad as it looks. Really. This is it." I gesture to my mouth, trying to reassure him, but it doesn't work.

My dad's forehead furrows as his entire face pinches.

"Is that Loveday? Is she okay?" Clarity appears over Royal's shoulder, and she gasps when she sees me. "What did he do to you?"

"What?" Lotus appears over Royal's other shoulder, his brown eyes taking me in. His head shakes from side to side as his lips pucker. "I'll kill him myself."

"Is Starling with you?" Clarity asks, her eyes peering past me.

"Yes, he's here."

Starling moves to stand behind me, one hand wrapped protectively over my shoulder. "I'm here."

"You let your slimy dad lay hands on her? You should be ashamed of yourself."

"Lotus!" Clarity's hand smacks him in the chest. "I'm sure he would have prevented it if he could."

"I would have. I'm sorry."

"Don't let it happen again, or we're gonna have words."

Over my shoulder, Starling nods.

Royal rubs a hand over his forehead. "Is there a reason for this call? I doubt Charles would allow you to call simply to chat."

"He wants us to remind you of your meeting today. And motivate you to come, on pain of my death."

"He's such a classy guy."

Clarity shoots another indignant look at Lotus, who ignores it, looking not at all chastened.

Julep moves into sight at Lotus's back, pulling him aside so she can see Royal's phone screen. Lotus tucks an arm around her shoulders, as if Julep is meant to be there, pressed to his side.

Julep sucks in a breath when she catches sight of my split lip, and her eyes flash. Glancing at Royal, she speaks. "We're nearby, okay? Don't worry. We're coming for you."

"Thanks." I look past them, searching for Haru, but she's nowhere to be seen.

"We'll see you soon," Julep says, lifting her chin confidently.

"Yeah." I end the call and chuck the phone at Darnay.

The man catches the device deftly, and returns it to his pocket. Then he pins a stony look on me. "How does it feel knowing you'll never speak to your father again?"

My fists clench as ice splashes through my veins.

The hours creep by so slowly that I could swear the digital

144

clock on the oven has stopped working. The metal heart of the clock mounted on the wall over the television has long since fallen silent. My hands rip through my greasy hair, and I pivot on my heel, following the same path back and forth in front of the windows that I've been pacing over for hours.

I throw back a swig of water from the paper cup Chopper provided, crumple it up, and drop it onto the ground.

Forty minutes until Royal is supposed to meet Darnay down in the park.

Forty minutes until our final showdown with Nexus. And my team is nowhere to be seen in the cemetery below, which is teaming with people.

"Hey," Starling says, reaching out to wrap his fingers lightly around my wrist. "He's going to be fine, and so are we. You have to know that."

"Fine like everyone else who's ever gotten in Nexus's way?" The words bite, but Starling doesn't flinch.

"I know it looks bad."

"Understatement of the year."

The clock clicks over to the half hour mark.

Thirty minutes to go.

My stomach is in knots so tight I'm not sure I'll ever be able to unwind them. I plop down onto the couch beside him, wondering if I should put a voice to the thoughts swirling around my head. I glance at Starling, who is watching me intently.

"Tell me what you're thinking," he prompts.

I take a deep breath, giving myself time to weigh my words. Once they're out, I don't know how Starling will respond, how deep my words will cut. I meet his eyes and plunge ahead. "So, obviously we're in your mom's family's old apartment, where she brought you when she came to visit, before she… died. And there's that park across the street. I've been thinking, and I'm pretty sure it's the park where your mom was killed. Have you seen that slide, over in the corner?"

Starling swallows as his eyes go to the window. "I have, and you're right. My father all but confirmed it when we spoke last night. One of the benches facing the park, right out there, is where my mother died. And her resting place is in the cemetery, next to my grandparents. I never got to see them, after."

"I'm so sorry. I can't imagine how it feels to be working with the man who, you know." My gaze drops to where my hands are balled in my lap.

It's quiet for a moment, and then Starling says, "I was shocked when I heard, when I realized what my father was saying, but it was so long ago. I guess what I'm trying to say is that it doesn't hurt as much as I thought it would. I feel a sense of loss, but it's not consuming like the pain my father seems to be feeling."

"So you're saying you're not going to channel it into a thirst for revenge?"

"Probably not."

"That's good to know." The sound from outside compels me toward it. Standing up, I cross to the window, hoping to be distracted by all of the hustle and bustle below. Voices filter through the closed window as families congregate around the resting places of their loved ones. The conflicting sounds of different radio stations clash, adding to the cacophony in my ears. I am glad Starling and I talked about how he's feeling; it makes me feel closer to him. But I'm still twisted in knots over my dad's fate. At this moment, his death seems almost inevitable. My hands clench into fists at my sides.

Starling pushes himself off the couch and wraps his arms

around me. "Everything is going to work out. You aren't going to lose your dad."

"You can't guarantee that." But his solid body and slow, even breaths are working their magic on my muscles, siphoning off the tension in my neck and shoulders. I snake my arms around his waist and rest my cheek against his chest. He smells mustier than normal, but I probably do too. Not showering for a couple of days will do that. My eyelids go heavy and my eyes slide closed.

"She's right, you know. You shouldn't make statements like that unless you can back them up."

I jump back from Starling like I've been shoved, my pulse throbbing in my ears.

Starling whirls around to face Darnay, who puts on a smile that's obviously disingenuous. He's showered and changed into a fresh suit, his jacket crisply pressed and his pants creased perfectly down the front of both legs. "Well, I must be going. Important meeting. Oh, and Loveday, I'm so sorry for your loss." He laughs, *actually laughs* as he makes his way toward the door. With one hand, he gestures for Rocket to follow him.

The door thuds behind them and Chopper slides the bolt into place. Then, he and Twister move toward us, drawing their weapons.

My feet widen to fighting stance, and my hands come up reflexively. We may be outgunned, but I'm not going anywhere without a fight.

Starling must agree, because his body moves into a similar form. "I thought you were going to let us go free, once this is over."

Twister gives him a hint of a smirk.

My heart lurches sideways. They aren't intending to let us go, at all. Eyes narrowed, I take a step back, studying our opponents. Maybe we can fight our way out of here.

"Put your hands behind your backs," Chopper orders.

My eyes flick downward to the coffee table, weighing my odds of being able to heave it toward Chopper and Twister before either of them can get a shot off. My mouth flattens into a tight line. There's no time.

"Put your hands. Behind your back," Twister growls, taking another heavy step toward us, his fingers on the holster at his waist.

Out of the corner of my eye I see Starling give the slightest nod.

Gritting my teeth, I comply with the order. In seconds, our hands are bound behind us by zip ties once more.

Twister yanks the strap around my wrists tighter and tighter, until it digs into my flesh. "Don't even think about doing something heroic," he says, "or we'll put bullets in your brains." With one large, rough hand, he shoves me toward the window. "The show's about to start."

Chapter 27

My body arches away from him, but the man is so close there's nowhere for me to go.

Chopper takes up position behind Starling, his gun held to the middle of the younger man's back.

Starling's eyes find mine again, and I can see the certainty there. He's confident we're all going to come through this experience mostly unscathed.

The tip of my tongue touches the raw skin of my lip. I'm not so sure.

In the corner of my eye, a flicker of white draws my attention. It's Royal, still wearing his white button up and slacks. His appearance is considerably more rumpled than the last time I saw him, but even so, he moves with sure steps over the sidewalk. For a moment, he looks up toward our building, and I can feel it down to my toes. He's looking right at us. I close my eyes against the press of Twister's gun barrel pointed at my head, and open them, hoping my dad will see the strength in my face.

But he's already looking away.

I can barely breathe as I watch him walk between the vendors lining the street, toward the small playground at the edge of the cemetery. He weaves in and out between the camping tents and canopies pitched around many of the graves, avoiding stepping on food offerings and photos that people have left for their deceased loved ones in preparation for All Saints' Day. Candles flicker at his feet as he passes a stone monument of a woman in prayer. The virgin Mary, maybe?

"You see that?" Twister growls in my ear. "Mr. Darnay knew your dad would show up, as long as we kept you here. Now all he has to do is sit quietly while Mr. Darnay shoots him."

His hot breath on my skin triggers my gag reflex, making me want to turn and wretch all over the disgusting man, but he's got a vice grip on my upper arms, holding me pressed against the window so I can see the slaughter. See it, but not be able to stop it.

Starling taps my foot with his own. "He'll get out of this, somehow. Your dad is smart. Trust him."

I shake my head, unable to stop the fear from mounting into my throat. "You don't understand. There's no way he'll raise a finger against Darnay while we're being held here. He'll let Darnay kill him, if it means we'll be set free. He won't see any other choice."

Twister chuckles. "You're cute, thinking we're going to let you go after your dad is dead."

Starling's eyes widen, and he pulls against Chopper's hands on his arms. "Let me go! You have to let us go. Those were your orders. My dad will—"

"He won't do anything once he's killed Royal. He won't care anymore. He'll have done what he came for, and he'll leave this chickie here to us." Twister cocks his head and gives a sadistic grin. "And she's the reason many of my squadmates are out of commission. I wanna return the favor."

A shudder runs through me. Everything he says is true. I have personally shot and injured quite a few of his teammates. And my teammates shot and captured who knows how many more at the airport in Atlanta. Torturing me would be an incredibly easy way to get his pound of flesh. My stomach churns at the thought. I twist and yank, hoping to loosen his grip on my arm, but he only squeezes tighter and presses me uncomfortably against the window ledge so that it digs into my gut, making it difficult to breathe deeply.

Down in the park, Royal crosses the last few steps toward the playground. He swivels his head to look around before navigating around the wooden bench and taking a seat at its center, facing the play equipment. No one has confirmed it, but I'd bet everything I have that it's the same bench where the authorities found Starling's mother, the day she was gunned down by Royal himself.

And if my team doesn't do something soon, it's going to become the very place where my dad, our dad, is killed as well.

My eyes dart over the park as I search, almost frantically, for any sign of Clarity, Lotus, or Julep. They're nowhere to be seen. Where are they? I know they didn't really let Royal go into the park alone, despite Darnay's demand, so where the hell are they?

A small child darts past the park bench where my dad is sitting and clambers up the steps toward the slide. A woman, presumably his mother, chases after him, stationing herself at the foot of the metal chute to watch him careen down, grinning wide as he flies off the end and into the woman's arms. Their matching black hair shines in the sun as they laugh with pleasure. Is that what Starling and his mom looked like on that terrible day?

Beside me, Starling has gone completely still, his eyes

unmoving as he watches. Thick, dark locks have fallen forward over his brow, making him look more boyish than ever.

I study his face, wondering if he's thinking the same thoughts as me.

"Starling, I…" My voice cuts off with a creak.

Slowly, he turns to meet my gaze. "I know." It's a whispered pardon for everything that has happened between us since we met, from my cold reception of him to the death of his mother at my father's hands. The blame for all of it doesn't rest at my feet, but I can take up the mantle of making reparations, and that's what I intend to do. Especially if my father doesn't survive his imminent encounter with Charles Darnay.

We stand in silence, watching the little boy climb up the steps and fly down the slide again and again, cared for by his effervescent mother. The weight of what could have been hangs heavy in the air. I should have stopped this, somehow. If only I had figured out that Darnay was Nexus mere minutes earlier.

A soft pfft interrupts my self-flagellation, and a second later Twister's hands drop from my arms. Chopper's gun drops to the carpet, and both of the goons collapse to the ground.

"What the …?" Starling spins, and a grin parts his lips.

I flip around in time to see Julep rushing toward me, stowing a tranquilizer gun as she moves. "Happy to see me?" she asks, pulling a small knife from her holster and moving behind us to cut the ties off our wrists. The plastic separates with a snip, and our hands are free.

"Just in time," I say, wrapping my arms around her in a quick hug.

Dropping to the floor, she uses a length of cord to bind the hands and feet of both Chopper and Twister in intricate knots that will take them quite a while to get out of. Once they wake up, that is. She straightens and meets my eyes. "What say we go rescue your dad?" Her mouth turns up in half a smile.

"I say that's the best idea I've heard all day." I smile back at her as she ushers us out of the room and toward the stairs. I ignore the pain in my leg as we run down the first flight of steps. I have to get to my dad before Darnay does, because knowing Royal, he won't brandish a weapon in a park filled with mourners and celebrants. The risk of hitting an innocent bystander with a stray shot is astronomically high. But Darnay? He won't hesitate. He's proven that he doesn't care about collateral damage as long as he gets his long-awaited revenge. I suck in a controlled breath, forcing my brain to ignore the pain radiating from my thigh. Instead, I push my muscles to move as quickly as I can, knowing that with every second that passes, my dad is farther from me, and closer to death.

Chapter 28

Starling bolts down the painted wooden stairs before pausing on the landing to look back and check on my progress.

I paste on a smile, but he must see through it because he takes a hesitant step up toward me.

Julep waves him on with an outstretched hand. "I'll stay with her. You go."

"Hurry!" I yell after him as he disappears out of the stairwell and around the corner.

"Come on," Julep says, shoving herself under my arm and propping me up on my injured side. "Let's get down to the park.

"What I wouldn't give for my crutch right now."

She chuckles under my weight.

"What? It was growing on me. It's like a walking aid and a fighting staff. Plus, people see it and automatically think I'm an easy target."

"Which you're not."

"Exactly."

The voices of the people gathered in the park across the street grow louder as we hit ground level. Warm afternoon sunlight streams through the glass panels in the door, lighting the hallway.

Julep sprints ahead to the door and holds it open for me. I maneuver around her, stepping gingerly on my injured leg. "Next time, remind me not to get shot."

"Don't get shot."

"Funny."

The door swings shut behind us and we're in the thick of it.

Vendors selling bouquets, flower petals, candles, and icons of all shapes and sizes envelope us as we make our way through the row of stalls lining both sides of the street. The tantalizing scents of fried foods waft over me, making my stomach growl. I'm all too aware of how long it's been since Chopper brought us that meager breakfast. After we rescue Royal I'm finding a litter and making Lotus and Starling carry me up and down the street so I can sample every single food I see.

But now, we need to hurry.

I scramble up the curb on the far side of the street, almost tripping over my own foot. Damn bullet wound is making my coordination jilted and slow. If someone were watching me walk they'd probably think I was a zombie.

"Here, take this." Julep thrusts a long and seemingly sturdy decorative parasol into my hands.

I don't question where it came from. "Thanks." It makes a surprisingly good cane, so I'm able to amble forward at a less undead-like pace. But we're still too far from the park where my dad is sitting, awaiting his execution.

We move through the throngs, careful not to step on the graves or upend the offerings that dot the grass near many of the stone markers.

A little boy eyes my use of the umbrella, then runs off toward a candy-striped canopy.

Laughter explodes from a green and silver camping tent to my left, making me jump. Take deep breaths, Loveday. Everything is going to be fine. My eyes flick to where Royal is still sitting on that blasted bench. Scanning beyond him, I frown. There's no sign of Darnay. I should be relieved, but knowing he's out there somewhere I can't see is almost worse. Like a tornado that hits without warning.

My feet stumble as I notice a young woman staring at me, marking my hurried movements and strained expression.

"Julep," I whisper-yell. "Slow down."

She glances at me over her shoulder.

I widen my eyes and tilt my head ever so slightly toward our observer, who is still following us with narrowed eyes. "Slow down," I mouth. "Be cool."

Julep raises her eyebrows, but does what I ask. We can't afford to draw attention to ourselves, even with Royal's life on the line. If anyone happened to spot any of the weapons Julep's got hidden on her person, there'd be a park-wide panic and we'd never get to Royal in time.

As I walk in the most carefree manner I can muster, considering I'm using a floral parasol for a cane and I'm limping like a three-legged elephant, I search the park. Where did Starling get to? And where are Lotus, Clarity, Haru, and Truly? They have to be here somewhere.

"Where is everyone?" I whisper to Julep.

"They're meeting us up ahead, at the giant cross monument."

I look where she's pointing and see it. Actually, it's kind of hard to miss. The giant marble cross sits on a concrete pedestal, smack in the middle of the park. Made of dull gray stone, the cross has got to be ten feet tall. From there, it's not far to the park, and its pedestal base will provide an ample amount of cover for us. I crane my neck, looking for our teammates, but there's no bit of afro peeking up over the statue's base. No flash of a shiny wig. No tightly pulled ponytail of black hair.

My blood chills. "This feels like a trap."

"It's not a trap," Julep whispers. "Darnay had no idea you planted a tracker on Starling. Genius, by the way."

"I wasn't sure if you'd find it in time."

Julep shrugs. "Haru found it. She may be cute, but I wouldn't get on her bad side. Girl could find a person's internet footprint even if they'd been dead since before computers were invented."

I glance over my shoulder, but the woman who was watching us has moved on. Hopefully not to call the authorities.

We creep over the grass toward the cross monument and move around the other side.

They aren't there, and there's no sign that they ever were.

"Are you sure this was the rendezvous spot?"

"Yes! We picked it because you can't miss it. It's huge."

"Hmm." I lean on the concrete base and peer over the top, toward the park. There are tents and canopies partially blocking my view, but I can just see the side of Royal's head and shoulder, still sitting on the bench facing the playset. Beyond him, there's no sign of any of our teammates. But I glimpse Darnay walking through the park along the opposite side, making his way toward the playground. My stomach clenches in apprehension.

Ducking behind the statue, I turn to Julep. "Do you know where Starling went?"

She peers up over the concrete block to look around, then ducks back down beside me. "I don't see him anywhere. Weird."

My pulse increases as paranoid thoughts invade my consciousness. "You don't think... It's not possible that he's been playing us the whole time, right? I would have seen that."

Julep shakes her head slowly. "You would have known. It's obvious to the rest of us that he's wild about you. You're like Starling catnip."

I can't help but smile at this. "It wasn't obvious to Royal, or Lotus."

She shakes her head. "Ignore Lotus. He was so upset at my being gone he needed a scapegoat."

"How do you know that?"

"We talked about it on the flight over. There was plenty of time."

"Sure."

"What'd we miss?" Lotus interrupts, hunkering down behind Julep.

"Any sign of Darnay yet?" Clarity asks over my shoulder. Peering over toward the playground, she stiffens. She must have caught sight of the man.

I, too, look in that direction. Darnay is picking his way through the green space toward the playground, his stealthy movements drawing no attention from the crowds around him.

"I'm glad you're okay, by the way," Clarity says. She wraps me in a tight hug before letting go. She takes another long look toward the playground. "Royal's still sitting there alone, but Darnay will be there in a minute."

"Yeah? I was hoping he would be a no-show."

Julep elbows Lotus lightly. "There's no way he wasn't going to show."

"We're not usually that lucky," I say. "Or at least not lately."

"What if I just go over there and ask Dad to leave? Maybe

158

he doesn't have to do this. He could still slip away before Darnay has a chance to hurt him."

I shake my head. "He won't go for it. Besides, if he doesn't face Darnay now, who knows what that revenge-thirsty maniac will do next."

Clarity nods, frowning. "I guess you're right."

"Think of it this way. In a matter of minutes, this will all be over." One way or the other. Only I don't say that. Clarity looks pale enough as it is, though to her credit that's the only outward sign that she's nervous. I swallow my own jitters.

"Where were you a minute ago?" Julep asks, looking at Clarity over my shoulder.

"We ran into a couple of Darnay's men, and we had to incapacitate them without making any noise. It turns out, that's not so easy."

Julep merely nods in solidarity.

I take a look over the top of the statue and my heart stops. Darnay is walking casually along the cement path surrounding the park, right toward Royal. He's got a large bouquet of flowers in one hand, and an unlit candle in the other. He must have stopped to purchase them on the way. What's he thinking? Kill Royal then visit his dead wife's grave, still basking in his triumph? Revulsion rips through me. How can he possibly think killing my father will give him peace?

My eyes run over Darnay again. There's a telltale lump under his shirt. I watch for a moment, hoping to see Starling somewhere in the crowd, but he's nowhere to be found.

"Where's Starling?" Lotus asks Julep. "Wasn't he with you?"

"He was, but he ran ahead."

"So. where is he?" A hint of suspicion has crept back into Lotus's voice.

Julep cocks her head at him, eyebrow raised. "I'm sure he knows what he's doing."

"Right…" Lotus trails off, sneaking a glance toward me.

I bite my lip and duck back down. "Guys," I hiss. "Darnay is almost to Royal. We have to do something without making a scene. Does everyone have a tranquilizer gun handy?"

All three of them pull a weapon from a hidden spot on their person: Lotus from a holster tucked into his waistband, Julep from the holster strapped to her thigh under her skirt, and Clarity from a holster strapped to her abdomen under her blouse. I can't help but grin. These are my people.

"All right then. Lotus and Julep, swing wide and come up behind Darnay. Clarity, come at him from the left. If any of you has a clear shot and can take it without being seen, do it. We have to incapacitate him before he draws his weapon. If anyone sees him it'll cause mass panic, which we need to avoid at all costs. Well, not at all costs. If at all possible, okay?"

Three heads bob in agreement, and then my teammates move out from behind the statue in the directions I indicated.

My eyes are glued to Royal, still sitting on the bench. It's clear from the angle of his head that he's spotted Darnay and is watching him approach.

Darnay, for his part, looks calm despite the anger that's seething in the depths of his soul.

A little girl squeals as she barrels down the slide into a teenage boy's arms.

Darnay barely spares a glance in their direction before returning his focus to my dad. His footsteps slow as he approaches the bench. He says something to Royal that I can't hear. I really should take up lip reading.

There's a flicker of movement behind a headstone to his right. A flash of white. It's got to be Clarity. Hopefully she has a shot.

"Come on, Clarity," I breathe. "Take the shot."

A pack of gleeful children run by me toward the playground.

My eyes widen. They're heading right for Darnay.

I grip the edge of the concrete statue base, hoping the man has the sense not to shoot my dad in front of a bunch of seven year olds.

Darnay doesn't even look at them as they take up residence at the water fountain, effectively blocking Clarity from taking out Darnay.

I blurt a curse word into the stone, and then swivel my head to study the park beyond Darnay. Where are Lotus and Julep? And where is Starling?

Quick as a blink, Clarity slides out from her hiding place and begins to maneuver around the kids to a new hiding place behind a vacated camping tent.

I refocus on Royal and Darnay. Royal hasn't moved, but Darnay is standing much closer to him now, his mouth morphing into a jagged, angry shape. The bouquet and creamy, wax candle sit on the end of the bench, all but forgotten.

I catch a glimpse of Lotus over Darnay's shoulder, but then he's blocked by an old lady strolling through the cemetery holding a giant, bright purple parasol. In her free hand, she's got some kind of meat on a stick and she's nibbling at it as she walks, her steps slow and relaxed. "Move, lady!" I want to yell, but instead I bite down on my tongue.

My stress level shoots through the roof. Of all the days to declare a showdown, Darnay had to pick All Saints' Day. He had to have known it would be nearly impossible for us to shoot him in such an open, exposed place. It's a diabolical plan, but it's working. I bite down on my lip. If I had a weapon, I might could get off a shot, but I'm woefully unarmed.

Darnay surreptitiously unsnaps the strap on his gun holster, poising his fingers to withdraw his weapon.

My heart leaps into my throat.

"High there, chickie." I gasp in shock as large hands clamp down on my shoulders and slam me into the concrete block. Twister's hot, stank breath washes over me. "Thought you'd get away so easily, didn't you?"

I attempt to get out of his hold, but he's got his full weight behind his arms, and I'm smashed against the solid gray surface. Its gravelly facade digs into my skin. "Let me go, asshole."

He chuckles. "No. Before, that was work. But this? This I'm doing for fun." There's something in his tone that fans the flame of fear in my belly until it's an inferno, blazing through my chest and out toward my fingertips.

When he speaks into his earpiece, his voice is more controlled. "Mr. Darnay? I've got the girl under control. Go ahead and take your shot."

Chapter 29

Wincing at the force of Twister holding me against the
concrete, I take stock of my position. I'm unarmed and being
held with my arms twisted roughly behind my back. The man's
broad hand rests in the center of my spine, holding me against
the man-made edifice. I suck in a breath at the pinch at my
wrists, and try to focus on where Royal is sitting on the park
bench.

I look around frantically, hoping for a sign of Clarity,
Lotus, Julep, or Starling. Where are they? And why haven't they
incapacitated Darnay by now? But it's easy to see why they're
being cautious. There are people everywhere, from newborn
babies all the way up to hunched over, wrinkly grandmas and
grandpas with dark hairs sticking out of their moles. People
may not be super observant, but they tend to notice when
someone pulls out a gun. Heck, one time Lotus got made by a
woman who saw him and mistook his tripod for a hunting rifle.
But that was back in the states, where people tend to be jumpy.
Still, I'm guessing the people here today won't be able to tell
the difference between the tranquilizer guns my teammates are
carrying and the real deal strapped to Darnay's side.

The air around me stills, causing me to straighten up, my

instincts humming.

"Let her go, now, or I'll put one in the back of your skull." It's Clarity, and it's the first time I've ever heard that tone of barely concealed rage.

Twister grunts, but then his hands ease away from my back and wrists.

"Get down on your knees," my sister growls.

I spin around to see Twister lowering his bulky body to the ground, and Clarity with her gun pointed square at the back of his head, concealed by a bouquet of flowers. Nice one, sis.

Once Twister complies, Clarity's eyes flit to me. "Disarm him and tie his hands and feet. I've got ties in my back pocket."

"Yes, ma'am," I say, the relief obvious in the relaxing muscles in my neck.

I make quick work of binding Twister, using the statue for some semblance of cover. Once I'm confident he's restrained, I search him, tossing all of his weapons and gear into the nearest garbage can. For once, I'm glad to see its filled with greasy fast food wrappers and uneaten bits of food.

"Don't move," Clarity says, voice low, "or I'll end you."

You know, she's kind of scary when she's like this. It's a shame she's giving up spy work for costume and makeup design.

Our eyes meet again as my sister stands rigid, holding the bouquet expertly out toward Twister. "Go. Save Dad."

"Thanks."

Then I'm scrambling through the graveyard, trying not to draw Darnay's attention.

Past the playground, I catch a glimpse of Julep and Lotus trying to reposition themselves to avoid the crowd that has gathered around another grave marker. Julep's face is tight in concentration, and Lotus's skin is beaded with sweat.

Royal is still sitting on the bench, waiting for Darnay to make a move.

Time seems to freeze as the man pulls out his gun, slowly and carefully, and aims it directly at Royal's heart, keeping it hidden in the flap of his jacket.

A snap under my feet makes me freeze. I've stepped on a tiny balloon on a stick. Damnit.

When I look up, my blood runs cold.

Darnay has spotted me. The corner of his mouth curls upward in an arrogant smile before his face drops to focus on Royal once more.

My eyes scan around for something, anything I can use as a weapon. The only things nearby are flowers and candles. I briefly consider chucking the lit pillars at him, but they'd be out by the time they reached him, and thus wouldn't actually light him on fire. Besides, the lumps of wax around me have been lovingly placed by people in remembrance of their fallen family members, and I'd hate to mess that up.

I don't dare look past Darnay to where I think Lotus and Julep are, for fear he'll make them as well. So instead I stand on the grass, not moving as I watch Darnay prepare to shoot my father, the only parent I have left.

There's a blast as someone nearby turns up their radio. The sudden loud noise is jarring, making me want to reach up and plug my ears.

Darnay flinches and looks toward the sound.

Starling jumps out from behind a nearby camping tent and sprints toward his dad, gun held close to his side in an attempt to avoid being seen.

My eyes widen at the scene and relief courses through me.

Before Darnay can react, Starling has the weapon pressed against his father's back, and the older man's entire body goes rigid. I'm not sure where he got the gun, but it doesn't matter.

Clarity moves up beside me. "I tranquilized…" But her words are hushed when she catches sight of Darnay pointing his gun at Royal, and Starling pointing his gun at Darnay. Behind his father, Starling's mouth is moving, but I'm too far away to hear what he's saying. I'm definitely learning to read lips once we get back to D.C.

"Come on," I say, taking her hand and pulling her forward. I have to know what Starling is saying right now.

With my sister's help, we near the playground and come to a stop a few yards away from where Royal, Darnay, and Starling are gathered. Royal's profile is visible to us from our position, and he peeks at us out of the corner of his eye. Then his focus returns to Darnay.

"Dad, put the gun down," Starling asks, the emotion plain in his voice. "You can't kill Royal. It won't bring Mom back."

Darnay huffs. "No, but it will make me feel better knowing her killer paid for his crime."

Starling doesn't move a muscle, doesn't remove the gun from his father's back. "It won't make you feel better. You've let this lust for revenge eat away at you for twenty years, but this won't make the pain go away."

"I have to avenge her death."

"If you do this, I'll shoot you."

"No, you won't," the older man says. "You don't have it in you."

Starling's jaw clenches. Maybe Darnay is right.

"I'll never forgive you."

Darnay's face lines in resignation. "So be it." He starts to squeeze the trigger.

"No!" I lunge forward, stumbling over a tree root and landing with a thud on my hands and knees. Tears well behind my eyes.

A faint pfft catches my attention. My muscles release at the familiar sound.

A tranquilizer dart lodges in Darnay's neck. His gun clatters to the ground as he swats at his neck, but he's crumpling to the grass before a second has passed.

Royal lunges forward and scoops up the surrendered handgun, securing it and pocketing it. Then he straightens and looks in the direction wence the dart came.

Lotus and Julep pop up from behind another monument, pleased smiles on their faces.

"You were cutting it pretty close," Royal says, smiling at them.

"Sorry, boss," Lotus says as he steps out from behind the stone edifice. "It turns out, finding a window in a crowd like this is trickier than I thought."

"It was a brilliant shot," Julep says, rubbing his back.

Clarity pulls me off the ground and we gather around Darnay's fallen form.

We've started to draw attention, so we need to move our two prisoners out of here quickly.

An older man approaches us just as Royal and Starling lift Darnay from the ground, bracing his limp form between them. The man says something to Royal in Filipino, and Royal answers, miming that Darnay has had too much to drink. The man doesn't look wholly convinced, but he doesn't argue. Turning away from us, he only glances back once before rejoining a group of people under a white canopy tent.

"Let's move, shall we?" Royal says.

"Can I get help with one of the Cobalt guys back that way?" Clarity asks.

Julep and Lotus nod and move off after my sister.

Royal raises his eyes to look at me. "Are you ready to go home?"

"You have no idea." I grin up at him, and we turn to leave the park.

"If it's all right, there's something I'd like to do first." Starling's words are hesitant, but his eyes don't flinch away from Royal.

"What is it?"

Starling licks his lips. "My mother, she was buried here, and I'd like to say goodbye."

Royal studies the boy for a moment. "I understand. Go ahead. Meet us at the rendezvous point. I'll send it to your watch."

"We don't have our watches."

Royal's eyebrows rise at this. "Oh, right." He takes his own watch off and hands it to me. It feels like a baton being passed, and I almost want to shove it back into his outstretched hand. Almost. But in truth, I've been training for this for six years, and I'm ready.

Starling shrugs off Darnay's arm and looks at me. "Will you come?"

"Yes."

Scooping the bouquet and cream-colored pillar candle off the bench, Starling moves over to me. He puts his free arm around my waist to support me, and together we amble through the park, back toward the place where he and I were held hostage, a mere half an hour ago.

He stops suddenly, and his eyes fall to a small stone marker that lies flat in the grass. It reads, *Maureen Marikit Sabio, Beloved wife and mother, 1987-2012.* Already there are several bouquets of flowers draped around the edges of the stone marker, and a candle flickers as we scoot closer.

"This is why I was late, back there. I stumbled over this, and I couldn't tear myself away."

I lean my head into his chest, not sure what to say.

He sighs. "It doesn't feel real, being here, looking at her grave after all these years."

I swallow the guilt that has risen in my own throat. I haven't been to my mom's grave in a very long time. "I'm glad I can be here for you. And maybe when we get back to D.C. we can visit my mom's grave, too."

He nods, not taking his eyes off his mom's name, etched in stone. Gripping the flowers and candle, he looks down at me. "He never brought me back here, you know. He always said it would be too difficult. I don't know if that was a lie, or the truth. And after today, I don't know if I'll ever find out." He kneels and places the flowers carefully against his mother's grave. Then he lights the candle on one of the others and sets it gently above his mother's name. When he stands up, I take his hand.

"I'm sorry he chose revenge over you, in the end."

Starling gives a slight head shake. "I didn't expect anything less."

"Still, I'm sorry."

Releasing a loud exhale, he squeezes my fingers. "Let's go meet the rest of our team."

The words warm me from my toes up to the crown of my head. He's right. It is our team now.

Chapter 30

I have never been so happy to be aboard an airplane as I am right now. In the cockpit, Pete and Lotus are handling her with expert precision, navigating over the globe toward home. It's kind of amazing, actually, that such a small aircraft can fly so far.

I glance toward the back of the plane, where Darnay, Rocket, Chopper, and Twister are slumped together. Each one is handcuffed wrists to ankles. And each one is unconscious. We may have dosed them with tranquilizer—enough to keep them out for hours, this time.

"Loveday, Julep, a word." Royal's face is serious, his forehead lined.

I pull myself out of my seat and hobble over to sit beside my dad.

Julep sits in the seat across from us and swivels it to face us.

He clears his throat. "I know you haven't always been in agreement with how I run this team, but I only did what I thought was best for everyone. I hope you understand that."

Julep inclines her head to one side, listening.

Royal focuses his blue eyes on her. "Going forward, you'll

all have to decide what you want to do, if continuing to work as spies is what you want. To that end, the agency is opening an organized crime unit in Los Angeles. From what I understand it will involve more long-term undercover assignments like the ones you excelled at when you were with the CIA. I've recommended you, Julep, to head up that office."

My mouth drops open in shock. He's going to try to transfer her, after all.

Julep's head shakes from side to side. "I thought you were okay with me and Lotus…"

"I'm not banishing you to California. I also recommended Lotus for a position there, if that is what the two of you want."

My eyebrows fly upward into my hair. This I was not expecting. I let my gaze flit to the window to avoid looking at Julep. I've been in charge for less than three minutes and already I might be losing people. But I keep my mouth shut. If Julep wants to go back into undercover work, she should do it, regardless of my feelings on the matter. And if Lotus chooses to go with her, so be it.

Julep's mouth widens into a smile.

Yep, I'm going to lose her.

"That's so sweet of you, but I want to stay here. Loveday and the rest have become like family to me, and it would be an honor to continue to serve with them."

"Really?" I blurt, before I can stop myself.

Julep reaches over and takes my hand, giving it a squeeze. "Really."

"And not just because I've got a hot guy on my team?"

Her eyes flash at my teasing before flicking toward the cockpit. "Not just because of that, but it does help."

I snicker. "I'll take it."

She laughs then, her loud, brassy laugh. I can't help but

laugh with her.

Everyone else turns to look at us, curious as to what has caused our outburst. Clarity arches an eyebrow at me in curiosity. I shake my head. She'll know everything soon enough, because we're not quite done yet.

I stand, rolling my shoulders. My entire body aches with fatigue, but we're not done yet. "If I can have your attention. Julep, can you borrow Lotus from Pete for a minute?" I wait as Royal, Starling, and Clarity focus on me. Julep moves up to the cockpit and returns with Lotus. They settle into chairs facing me. It turns out that Haru and Truly stayed behind to keep an eye on Julep's grandma while the rest flew to the Philippines. It was probably a good call.

I look at my sister. "Can you call Haru, get her in on this? I have something important to say."

"Just give me a second." She pulls out her tablet and swipes at the screen.

Haru picks up on the first ring. "Hello? Is everyone there? Is everyone okay?"

"We're fine." Clarity smiles down at the screen.

"Turn it around, will you?"

She does.

I lick my lips, glancing down at Royal's watch on my wrist. We have six hours before we land, which isn't a lot of time. I get right to the point. "As you all know, Royal is retiring, and I'll be leading this team moving forward. It should be obvious to everyone that Royal and I have some different opinions when it comes to how this team should be run."

Julep shakes her head in amusement.

Clarity smiles.

"We've always been taught to keep our personal lives secret, to protect each other and make sure that our families

172

didn't become a liability, but after everything we've seen with Darnay, I don't think that's the best policy anymore. And with that in mind…" My eyes land on my sister, silently asking her if she's ready to share her biggest secret.

She nods in affirmation. "Royal is my biological father," she says.

"What?" Haru cries, her voice sharp over the tablet's speakers. "I didn't know that!"

Lotus's eyebrows fly upward. "I'm shocked."

"We were too," I say, "when we found out."

Julep's face is wide with surprise as she tries to process this. "So, espionage really is a family business, huh?"

I grin. "Yep. Anyone else want to clear the air?"

Lotus shuffles his feet. "I'm in love with that girl right there." He blushes and points at Julep.

Royal's lips split, and he actually laughs. "We know that already."

Julep looks particularly pleased at this. She toys with her fingers in her lap and beams at Lotus.

"And there's something else… I have a younger brother back in Chicago. I worry about him, a lot."

My eyebrows rise. This I did not know. "We'll check on him, once we're done with this job. Okay?"

Lotus meets my eyes. "That would mean a lot. Thanks, sis."

Clarity's mouth forms a small O at this, and I break into a smile. "Come here." I gesture with both arms, beckoning Lotus toward me. He walks over and gives me a loose and very quick hug before letting go. He pats Clarity's shoulder and returns to his seat. Julep takes his hand and intertwines their fingers. The smile he gives her nearly makes my heart burst.

"Aww, how cute," Haru squeals. "I have something," she

blushes. "I miss my parents and I might want to go home, but I don't know. You all have done so much for me, and you've all become my very best friends, and I don't know what I would do with Baron while I was gone." She gets it all out in a rush, then takes a deep breath.

I glance at Royal, who clears his throat. "Loveday already asked me about sending you home for a couple of weeks, but I had a better idea. To thank you for your service to our country, the United States would like to offer your parents citizenship. If it's okay with you, we'll fly them over next week."

"Really?" Haru squeals through the tablet. "Thank you, thank you, thank you! If I was there, I'd give you a big hug!"

He gives her a polite smile. "That won't be necessary. You're welcome."

She stoops out of the frame and pops back up, holding Baron toward the camera. The cat yowls. "Do you hear that Baron? Mom and dad are coming to live here. Don't worry; Daddy will love you. And I'll work on Mom."

Starling lifts a hand. "I've got one. My real name is…"

I can see Royal clenching his jaw, but to his credit he keeps his mouth shut. It looks like he's really going to let me run the team as I see fit, no matter how much it goes against his instincts.

"Armando Sabio."

Clarity giggles. "Your real name is Armando? How very not English."

Royal groans.

"Armando Sabio." I whisper the name, trying out how it feels on my tongue. I like it.

Starling bobs his head toward Clarity. "My mom was Filipino, and I use her last name."

She grins. "It suits you."

174

"Anyone else?" I ask.

My team dissolves into a mass of chatter, which I allow. It's a good mental break from our mission. Everyone talks over each other for another minute before I call everyone to attention.

"As fun as this has been, we have a job to finish. We may have caught Nexus, but there's one more thing we have to take care of before we're finished." I turn to Lotus. "Can you check with Pete, see if we have enough fuel to fly a little longer than we had planned?"

Lotus's eyebrows push together. "I can ask. Where do you have in mind?"

My eyes slide to Clarity, because this last part of our mission is for her.

"Boston."

Julep sits up straight in her seat, lips parting. When she meets my gaze, it's clear she knows exactly what I'm talking about.

"We have..." I look down at my watch. "Maybe eight hours until we land in Boston, and we're going to need every minute of that time to prepare. Julep, can you fill us in on everything you know about the Sicilian mob in the area?"

"Yes, ma'am."

"Here we go," Lotus says.

And he's kind of right. Here we go.

Chapter 31

"Call your uncle. Use this." I toss the burner phone to Clarity, who catches it like she does everything else—like she's incapable of any movements that don't make her look like a ballet dancer.

"You want me to call him, now?" Her large eyes shine up at me.

"Yeah. Let's see what he has to say for himself."

She nods and dials the number.

Honestly, I'm expecting him to deny he had any involvement in the ambush at the airport in D.C., but that might just be my distrustful, cynical nature talking. And it's about time I try trusting others, even if just a little bit.

Clarity scurries into the airplane bathroom for some privacy, and I don't blame her.

I'm tempted to follow her, listen in on the no-doubt awkward conversation she's having, but that trust I mentioned? It should definitely extend to my sister, so I hang back, waiting for her to come out with her verdict.

Julep watches from her seat, hands folded in her lap. The only indication that she's nervous at all about returning to Boston after all this time is the way she smooths her skirt every couple minutes. I wonder if she's thinking about her former partner, Sean. Honesty? I'd be nervous if I had to go back to the place where Vale was killed. What sort of memories is setting foot in Boston going to dredge up for Julep? Will images of Sean be all she can see? I push the questions away. Julep is a professional, and I'm choosing to believe that she won't allow painful memories to impede her decision-making on the ground. Trust.

The plane sways under my feet, sending a wave of movement up through my core that makes me bob to one side. Not ready to sit down, I widen my stance.

Starling takes a sip of the cup of water in his hand, eyes focused on Darnay, who is still unconscious at the back of the plane.

"Hey. Are you okay?" I wait for Starling to meet my eyes.

With effort, he drags his attention away from his father and looks at me. "I'm all right. It's just going to take some getting used to, having my father in prison." He takes a deep, cleansing breath.

"It's not quite the same, but I can empathize. Discovering I had an aunt, and then finding out she'd been involved with, you know, it was a lot to deal with."

Starling finishes off his water and sets his cup on the tray table in front of him. "How did you deal with it?"

"I leaned into the people I knew were on my side. Clarity, Lotus, Julep... You. And pizza. Lots of pizza."

He grins at this. "I'll have to try your method. It sounds promising."

The bathroom door slides open and Clarity emerges, relief painted across her face.

"Well?" I prompt her.

"Uncle Nestore says they've been resistant to his efforts to legitimize their business right from the start. He told me he had no idea the Boston branch was planning to attack us to avenge Beppe Arnoni's arrest. He said he just found an app on his phone. He said they must have installed it without him knowing, and used it to trace my signal the last time we spoke. That's how they found us."

"So, he's got at least one leak there in Palermo he'll have to plug." I inhale deeply. "You believe him?"

She nods. "Yes."

"All right then." I hold out my hand, and she deposits the burner phone in my palm. Turning it over, I shut it off and take the sim card out. "Until this is over, only call Uncle Nestore on burner phones, and only use each one a single time before you ditch it. We can't risk another surprise. The only reason we made it out last time was because Julep recognized their guys at the last second. Did you tell your uncle to delete the app, and put a passcode on his phone?"

"Yeah."

"Then that takes care of that. Julep, you're up." I take my seat beside Starling and wait for Julep to begin briefing us on the Boston branch of la nostra società. We'll need all of the information we can get our hands on, and some good old fashioned luck. If it were me, I wouldn't be terribly keen on new agents showing up to my home and telling me they wanted in on the action, and I'm guessing the CIA boys on the ground in Boston are going to feel pretty much the same way.

Julep arranges a meeting with Gavin, the ranking officer on the ground in Boston, so as soon as we've landed, she and I leave the airport and catch a ride-share into the heart of downtown, where gastropubs and seafood places reign. Multi-story red brick buildings line the streets, and sapling trees are planted at intervals along the sidewalk, each one's base protected by a scalloped wrought iron barrier.

It's midafternoon, and the roads are lined with cars. People go in and out of the businesses carrying shopping bags and takeout containers.

I glance down at my watch to remind myself what day it is. I'm starting to lose track. How long has it been since Darnay attacked the Ivory Tower? A week? And how long since I had a shower? I sneak a whiff of my armpit, but Julep catches me.

"Don't worry about it," she says with a chuckle. "Gavin's no stranger to the job, and how it's a grind sometimes."

"That's good, because I'm pretty sure I don't smell great." At least I was able to use some toothpaste Clarity had, and brush my teeth with my finger. I run my tongue over my teeth. They feel clean and slick, unlike the rest of me. Catching a glimpse of myself in the mirror, I halt. I look rough. My bleached hair is greasy and clings to my scalp. There are dark circles under my eyes that would rival a raccoon's, and my mouth is bruised from where Darnay sucker-punched me. I let out a low whistle.

"Come on," Julep says, hooking her arm through mine and propelling me forward. "We're almost there.

The streets are bustling with cars as they whizz past us.

Julep weaves us expertly through the crowd without jostling into other pedestrians. It's like she's engaged her stealth mode and is using it to avoid drawing any attention to us. I like it.

We round the corner of a red brick building and stop under a sign that reads, "Edna's Crab Shack."

Unhooking her arm from mine, she looks me in the eyes. "Are you ready?"

I nod.

"Good. I'm not sure how Gavin will respond when we tell him why we're here. He was surprised enough when he got my call. Just, play it cool, okay?"

"Yes, ma'am."

She shakes her head at my sass, and then opens the door and ushers me inside.

The interior of Edna's Crab Shack is well lit by hanging lamps with red glass shades. Below each one is a picnic table covered with a red and white checked table cloth made of paper. It's almost 14:00, so the lunch crowd has dispersed, leaving the restaurant almost completely empty. We're greeted by a teenage girl wearing a white polo shirt, a name tag reading Kayla, and a hat shaped like a bright red crab, complete with pinchers, beady black eyes, and thick eyebrows.

My own eyebrows rise as I stifle a laugh.

"Welcome to Edna's Crab Shack. Table for two?"

"Actually, we're meeting a friend." Julep looks over the hostess's shoulder. "He's seated over there."

Kayla steps aside, still smiling. "Go right ahead, then."

We skirt past her and weave our way to the back corner of the restaurant, where a lone, approximately thirty-year-old man is seated in a corner booth nursing a glass of a brown liquid I'm hoping is flat soda. He's got shaggy brown hair that falls over his forehead. Thick, dark eyebrows are pulled down over deep-set green eyes, and he hasn't shaved in a couple of days, leaving dark stubble along his jaw and chin.

The man pushes to a stand when he sees us and slides out of the booth to give Julep an awkward side hug. "Nia, I'm surprised to see you. Who's your friend?"

"Gavin, this is Loveday. We've been working together for the past year on the Nexus case."

Gavin runs his eyes over me quickly before returning his focus to Julep. "I heard something about that. Have a seat."

We settle into the booth and a waitress comes to take our orders.

Once she's gone, we all go quiet.

Gavin takes a drink of his unidentified brown drink and sets it back down. "What brings you back to Boston? You were pretty cryptic over the phone."

Julep smooths her wrinkled skirt and meets his eyes. "As you know, we've been working on capturing Nexus and securing the CIA against attack."

"Which we did," I put in.

Julep casts a glance at me before continuing. "While we were on that case, we got entangled with Beppe Arnoni's organization in Palermo, and we had a run in with their Boston branch a few days ago. I'm sure you've heard about it."

Gavin nods, his face blank. "I'm aware. It was all the boys could talk about down at The Tapper."

"What's The Tapper?"

Gavin's eyes move to me. "It's essentially home base for the Sicilian mafia contingent here in Boston. I'm a bartender there. Have been for four years." He tilts his head. "What I want to know is, why are the two of you here?"

"As I said, we got tangled up with Arnoni's men once they discovered that a member of our team is actually his biological granddaughter.

Gavin's mouth drops open. "What?"

"That was my reaction too."

Julep pats my knee. "Anyway, we'd like to help you take down the rest of their men here in Boston, so they can't come after our teammate again. She's afraid they'll try to kidnap her again, and we want to prevent that from happening."

Gavin's expression hardens, and he runs a hand over his mouth. "You're telling me that you're back here, after disappearing two years ago, mind you, because you want to insinuate yourself into my investigation? And you think we can just bring down the entire Sicilian mafia in Boston, like that?" He snaps his fingers.

"I know it's not going to be easy—"

"You don't know shit. Things have changed since you've been gone, since Sean died."

"Then bring us up to speed."

But he's already shaking his head, pushing to stand up. "No thanks. I'm sorry for your teammate, but I can't help you. There's no place for you in our investigation. It was nice to see you, Nia. Nice to meet you, too… Have a nice day." Without even a backward glance, Gavin strides out of the restaurant and up the sidewalk.

The waitress arrives then, holding our steaming plates piled high with seafood and corn on the cob. "Is your friend coming back?"

Julep tears her eyes away from the door to look up at her. "No, I don't think he is."

I look down at my food, trying to push away the unease in my stomach. I knew it would be a tough sell without Gillian Harris backing us, but I didn't think we'd be shut down completely.

"What next?" Julep asks as she ties a bib around her neck and picks up her mallet.

"Lunch, and then plan b."

Picking up a crab leg, I wave it in the air. "Do you want to do the honors, or shall I?"

"Be my guest." She's grinning, and so am I.

Chapter 32

My recent involvement in the capture of Nexus has given me some pull with the higher ups at the CIA, because when I called to request a complete file with all of their information on the Sicilian mob in Boston, they sent over everything they had, including a dossier on our friend, Gavin. Which is why I'm waiting for him outside his apartment at 08:00 after having spent most of the previous day running around the city attempting to get our bearings.

The morning is cold, so I'm glad I've got my trench coat wrapped around me and hands deep in my pockets. It's fresh and clean, like me. Who knew that a laundromat and a shower could make a girl feel brand spanking new. "I'm in position."

"We are too," Lotus says through the comms. "Think he'll come this way?"

I crane my neck to look up at the second story, where there's a light shining in the window of the apartment facing the street. Gavin is due to meet his handler in fifteen minutes, and he's missed the last two meetings. If I was a suspicious person, I'd wonder if he had gotten in so deep with the mob that he had forgotten what he was doing in Boston in the first place. In any case, I'm hoping he doesn't blow off this meeting, because I just need a minute of his time to convince him that he needs our help.

The light in his apartment goes out.

"We're about to find out. He's coming out now."

The wood and glass door swings open and Gavin emerges wearing a black leather jacket with the collar popped. One hand hangs at his side, and in his other hand is a small package.

"Nice to see you again, Gavin." I fall into stride beside him, my entire body relaxed. Hopefully Gavin will pick up on my non-threatening vibe.

"Hey… you. What are you doing here?"

He's forgotten my name already. Nice. "I just came to have a chat with you. About the mob." I lean in to whisper these last words in a faux-conspiratorial manner. "Got a minute?"

"No, now's not a good time. I'm meeting someone."

"Your CO, I hope. From what I've heard, you've missed your last two check ins with him. Is there something you're not telling him, Gavin? Something I should know?"

His jaw clenches and his eyes flash in anger. "I don't have anything to tell you. You're just a kid. Go away." He surges forward, walking as quickly as he can away from me, clutching the brown package under his arm tighter now.

I jog to catch up. "What's in the package? Are you sending a birthday gift to your mother?"

Gavin halts on the sidewalk, his expression incredulous. "How do you know it's almost my mother's birthday?"

I give him a snide smile. "I know everything, Gavin. So, what's in the package?"

He narrows his eyes at me and takes off running up the sidewalk.

I roll my eyes and watch his progress, tapping my foot

casually. Amateur.

Gavin dashes away from me, rounds the corner, and lets out a yell.

Julep forces him backward into my line of vision, flanked by Lotus and Clarity. "Going somewhere?" she asks.

Sneaking up behind the man, I snatch the package out of his hand and rip it open, not exactly sure what I'll find. Maybe I don't know *everything*. Maybe it was a bluff. But I know enough. Inside, there's a stack of U.S. currency. A very big stack.

Gavin goes still, his hands dead weights at his sides, his eyes fastened on the sidewalk.

"Oh Gavin," I say, shaking my head. "You weren't on your way to visit the mayor by any chance, were you? To pay him off for awarding city contracts to mafia-run businesses? Because that would be bribery, and punishable by fifteen years in prison."

"It's not a bribe. It's gratuity, which is only punishable by a maximum of two years."

"Not according to the mayor."

Gavin's eyes widen. "You, you spoke to the mayor?"

I shrug.

He crumples in on himself. "What do you want?"

"All I want is to help you dismantle the mafia here in Boston. Would that be so bad?"

He glares at me, but by his silence I know I've got him over a barrel.

Smiling, I look at Clarity. "Let's take our friend here back to his apartment, and figure out our next step, shall we?"

Lotus and Julep frog march Gavin back to his apartment with Starling, Clarity, and me right behind them.

A biting wind brushes over us, making my sister shiver and hunker further down into her turtle-neck sweater. "Brr, it's cold," she says, shivering.

Gavin uses his electronic key to open the door to the building, and Clarity pushes past him into the warm interior. One by one, each of my teammates goes inside until I'm left standing alone. I pivot on my feet, sweeping the street for any sign that we've been seen.

Starling sticks his head out the door. "You coming?"

"Yep." I follow him inside, securing the door behind me. As we climb the stairs to Gavin's second story apartment, my feet feel lighter than they have in weeks. We are within striking distance of finishing something that started over a year ago, with what we thought was a simple car theft ring. Together, my team has journeyed all over the world and weathered loss, betrayal, damaging secrets, and so much more. As I look up the stairs to where my teammates are waiting outside Gavin's door, pride seeps into my chest. We've become so much more than we were as individuals. We've become a team, a family. And once we've broken the hold the Sicilian mafia has on Boston, and their ties to Nestore Arnoni's organization, we'll all be free to move forward, whether that means continuing to work for the CIA, retiring, or going to art school. The path we've been on for the past year leads to only one conclusion. A final showdown with Beppe Arnoni's men feels as inevitable as did our final confrontation with Nexus. And we're going to win, one more time.

Clarity catches my eye and winks. She's excited we're so close to the finish line. A pain cuts through me, but I know it'll lessen with time. Once we're done here, Clarity will be able to live her dream, even though it's not the same as mine.

Chapter 33

Gavin's place is pretty much what I expected from an undercover agent who lives alone and only comes home to sleep. The white walls are bare. The only furniture in the living room is a sagging futon, it's black cushion torn in one corner and leaking fluffy white stuffing. There's a pile of takeout containers overflowing from the garbage can in the kitchen, and water rings on the wooden coffee table. He couldn't pay me enough to go into the bathroom.

"What is going on with you?" Julep asks from where she sits on one end of the futon.

Gavin sits at the other end picking at the leaking stuffing with his thumb and pointer finger. A long thread of the fluff comes out of the cushion, and he drops it onto the floor. "About three months ago, my son," he swallows, " was diagnosed with cancer. I'm here, so I wasn't much help with all of the appointments. My wife had to do everything, and she, her boss fired her for having to take so much time off. We were already drowning in credit card debt." He draws a rough hand down the length of his face, still staring at the dingy tan carpet. "I was so close to convincing Angelo Marchetti to turn and testify against his boss, the head of the organization here in

Boston, but I, I…"

"You needed the money," I say, my tone confident.

"They pay me a lot more than the CIA does, and we were barely making it before. Now, with Dylan's cancer, we just… I regret it. I know I screwed up, but it felt like I didn't have a choice, you know?" He looks up at Julep, pleading with his eyes for her to understand.

"Bless your heart. I might have done the same thing if I was in your position." It's a lie carefully told, and Gavin buys it.

He sags back against the futon and shifts his attention to me. "All I need is some leverage over Marchetti, and I'm almost positive he'll agree to testify against his boss, but I've had some trouble getting anything incriminating enough. He's slippery, and he usually sends someone else to get their hands dirty so he has plausible deniability."

"What did you have in mind?" I ask, leading him.

"Evidence he'd laundered money, or been part of their drug distribution process, or—"

"Video of him threatening the mayor with a gun if he doesn't give them the state contracts they want?"

Gavin's mouth drops open as I take a phone out of my pocket and toss it to him. "Check out the photo album on there."

His fingers move over the screen, and a video starts to play.

"You'll award Marchetti Construction the contract, or you'll regret it." There's a sound of a gun cocking. A man gasping in surprise.

"What are you doing?" the mayor cries. *"Please don't shoot me. My family…"*

"I'm not going to shoot you. Consider this a warning."

Gavin's eyes fly up to mine. "How did you get this? Marchetti never does his own dirty work. He usually has Leoni or Falco do stuff like this."

I smirk. "If you want a job done right, you have to do it yourself."

Lotus laughs at Gavin's confused expression. "The police got an anonymous tip about a cat house across town just after Leoni and Falco went inside. So Marchetti didn't have anyone he trusted to send to the mayor's house. Which meant he had to go himself."

"And since we'd already bugged the mayor's office…" I shrug, pleased with how our plan is working out.

A smile rises to Gavin's lips. "Devious. I like it."

"So now all you have to do is convince Marchetti to testify against his boss, and we'll put his family into WITSEC. Think you can handle it?"

He studies me, eyes gleaming. "I may have underestimated you."

"Get in line."

Eight hours later, Gavin pulls into the lot in front of Quattro Formaggi, a local pizza place, and kills the engine. An employee runs out of the building clutching a bright red warming bag, tosses it into his car, and peels out of the lot.

"That guy takes deliver way to seriously."

Gavin chuckles.

"What's with mobsters and pizza places, anyway?"

Gavin glances at me from the driver seat. "They're Italian. It's what they know."

"It's so cliché. They should try to be more original."

"You don't like pizza?"

"I didn't say that."

His face turns serious. "You ready?"

I double check one more time to make sure my gun is in place in the holster strapped to my thigh, and meet his eyes. "Let's do this. Guys? We're going in."

"We're in the alley if you need backup," Lotus says over the comms. "And don't forget the safe word."

"Have I ever?"

Opening the car door, I step out, testing my weight on the scary-high stilettos Clarity procured for me. Goosebumps cover my arms and legs as I reach down to pull the slinky black dress I'm wearing down as much as possible over my thighs, but then the strapless top rides down. Stupid dress. The curly blond strands of my wig brush my shoulders, providing some cover from the frosty evening air.

Coming around the vehicle, Gavin slings an arm around me. My nose wrinkles at the cologne we used to douse his clothes. Together, we sway as we walk toward the pizza place, him leaning to whisper into my ear, and me giggling like crazy.

Royal was pissed when I told him I intended to go in with Gavin, but what other option did I have? I couldn't send Julep or Clarity in, because anyone from the organization might recognize either one of them, and really, what's more cliché than a sleazy guy dating a much younger girl who's way out of his league? Marchetti will eat it up.

My high heels catch on a crack in the asphalt, and I almost fall over.

Gavin's hand wraps tightly around my waist, holding me in place.

I giggle up at him. "That was so embarrassing."

"Naw, I got you."

I send a gooey grin his way and lean my head on his shoulder. "You're such a sweetie."

Gavin's hand sinks a little too low on my hip as we walk.

"Hand," I hiss, still keeping the love-sick smile on my face.

"Sorry." He pulls up so his fingers are grazing the small of my back as we reach the door to the restaurant. "Just getting into character."

Over the comms, Starling snorts.

"That line doesn't work on me," I whisper.

Gavin holds the door open for me to step inside.

The interior is busy with movement. Most of the tables are occupied by groups ranging from parents with small kids to older couples. And in the back corner, Marchetti is holding court with three other guys, a half-eaten pepperoni pizza on their table.

"It's nice and warm in here," I coo, rubbing at my freezing bare arms. "Where's your friend?"

"Shh," Gavin says under the loud music. "In the back." He prods me forward with his hand, leading me toward Marchetti's table.

Ruffling my hair, I sneak a glance at our target, and my pulse speeds. Marchetti and his men have already seen us and are watching intently as we advance toward where they are seated. As we draw close, Marchetti gestures, and two of the men stand up, vacating chairs facing him.

"Gavin, have a seat," the man says.

One of Marchetti's thugs puts a hand on my shoulder, pushing me down into the chair. It's not the greeting I was hoping for. Still, I keep my smile in place and take the proffered seat.

"I wasn't expecting to see you this evening," Marchetti says once we've taken our seats. He looks down his nose at us, his expression guarded.

Gavin looks up at the two men standing at our backs, and then meets Marchetti's gaze. "I just wanted to let you know I made the delivery you asked me to. No problem."

"Good. I might have another job for you, in a few days."

"Great. Look, can we get a minute? Alone?"

Marchetti's eyes flick to his men before returning to Gavin. "Whatever for?"

"I, uh, have something to ask you. It's not a big deal."

"If it's not a big deal, why must it be a private conversation?"

The men behind us take a subtle step forward, closing off our exit.

My fingers drift down to the hem of my skirt, just in case.

"Please. Marchetti. I just need five minutes of your time."

Marchetti picks up a napkin and wipes his greasy fingers. "Do you know what I like about you, Gavin? You get things done quickly, and without a mess." He slides out of his chair and stands, straightening his jacket. "Unfortunately, you're also a cop. Goodbye, Gavin." He turns to leave, and his men hem us in. One of them clamps a hand on my wrist.

Revulsion builds in my chest, but I ignore it, willing my face to keep it's shocked expression.

Another man clamps a hand on Gavin's shoulder. And that's when I see the handgun he has pressed to Gavin's back, obscured from the other diners by the man's broad form. When did he draw a gun?

"Wait! How can you say that? I'm not a cop." Gavin raises his empty hands toward Marchetti, but the man doesn't blink.

"Did you think we wouldn't see the group of them at your apartment this morning? They're all a little young, I grant you, but the way they carried themselves. I could spot a fed in a snow storm." His eyes rove over me. "And your girlfriend here, she's too young for you. Take them out back." With those parting words, he strides through the restaurant and out the

192

front door, leaving Gavin and I alone with his goons.

I swallow down the bile that has risen in my throat. This is not going how I thought it would go. If Marchetti was considering turning state's evidence, he doesn't seem to be now. He's got one heck of a poker face.

The man who has a hold on my wrist shoves me forward toward the hall at the back of the restaurant, heedless of the possible witnesses.

"Wait. Please. Let me go!" I whine, pulling at my wrist with frantic movements.

Gavin scuffles against the man who's pushing him forward, but neither of us makes any headway.

I shoot a glance toward the diners in the restaurant, but if anyone is observing what's going on back here, they aren't doing anything about it.

Panic builds in my chest. We were so stupid to walk into a mob-owned restaurant and expect social mores to keep Marchetti from making a move against us in broad daylight. What were we thinking?

We're mere feet away from the back door now, and the man holding me has also pulled a weapon.

My shoes screech along the linoleum floor as I struggle ineffectually against my captor. I yank against his grip, but I'm not able to get purchase. For once, my diminutive size is against me, and I can't use any of my self-defense training in the sight of all of the pizza place's patrons. Taking a deep breath, I try to calm my nerves.

Once they get us out that back door...

Chapter 34

Gavin tries to brace himself against the wall to block the men from taking us out back, but he can't resist a man who is pointing a gun at his gut. His green eyes meet mine. "I'm sorry about this. I didn't think he would do this. I thought he was close to agreeing to testify. And now we're both going to—"

"Don't say it. This can't be the end." But I don't know what else it could be. It certainly doesn't look good for us.

My pulse is frantic as the man pointing his gun at Gavin gestures for me to open the back door and step outside.

Biting my lip, I comply. The door squeaks as I open it and step into the darkened alley beyond, a gun pointed at my back.

Gavin and his man step out as well, and the door slams shut behind us.

I blink as my eyes adjust to the dark. My mind is scrambling. I doubt I could get my gun out of the holster on my thigh before one of Marchetti's men shoots me, so I'll have to try something else. My eyes scan the alley, but there's not much here. To my left, there's a large metal dumpster, but I'd have to get past both of the thugs to reach it. The corner of the building is maybe twenty yards to my right, but again, I'm not sure I could get there before one of them shot me.

I turn toward the man nearest me and look up into his cold, brown eyes. Maybe if I flutter my eyelashes he'll relent.

He doesn't.

"Climb into the dumpster, nice and slow."

I open my mouth to argue, but his fingers slide toward the trigger, cutting off whatever I might say. Instead, I nod, letting out a forced sob, and stumble toward the big green bin. The man at Gavin's back shoves him forward into me, and we both fall into the side of the garbage can.

"Get in."

Gavin lifts me up and helps me into the bin. My high heels pierce a takeout container as I sink, and its contents ooze out, issuing a foul smell that assaults my senses. My eyes start to water. The stench of rotting food envelopes me, making my stomach turn. Why is it always rotten food in these things?

Gavin hoists himself over the side of the bin and tumbles in beside me, landing in a pile of old lettuce. Bits of moldy green stick to his elbow as he pushes to a stand. Reaching over, he takes my hand before fixing a cold stare on our captors. "You don't have to do this. We'll leave. We'll disappear, and we won't cause any trouble."

"You're right. You're going to disappear."

I gulp. "Please, let me go. I had no idea my Gavin was involved with you guys. I don't even know your names. I won't say anything."

Gavin turns on me, eyes wide at my betrayal. But I keep going.

"Please," I plead, allowing desperation to seep into my voice. "I'm only twenty years old. I'm not even done with college yet. Gavin's too old for me anyway. Just let me…" My expression is wild, my eyes burning with unshed tears as I try to step toward the edge of the bin.

"Don't move." Retrieving a suppressor from his pocket, the man screws it onto the barrel of his gun. They're not as quiet as the movies make them out to be, but with the loud music playing in the restaurant, it's possible no one inside will hear the shots being fired.

My heart slams against my ribcage as my eyes skitter over the alley, looking for any signs of my teammates, but they're nowhere to be seen. I sob. "But I'm too young to die." The safe words.

The mobster rolls his eyes at his partner before raising the gun and pointing it directly at my chest.

I suck in a breath. This is it.

Gavin squeezes my hand tight.

"Freeze!" A loud voice yells out from somewhere behind us, sending elation through me.

"Duck!" I pull Gavin down into the dumpster just as Marchetti's men open fire. The bullets fly over our heads, the sounds muffled but still audible enough to make my ears ring.

Shots fly over the garbage bin. My teammates are returning fire!

One of Marchetti's men falls to the ground with a grunt. The other peeks over the dumpster and fires a few more rounds.

The air in the alley grows still as Marchetti's man hunkers down behind the end of the dumpster, trying to shield himself from his partner's fate.

I crawl toward that end of the garbage bin, trying to ignore the sticky bits of food that cling to my hands. I come up with a stale baguette. Shoving it aside, I push forward until I'm mere inches away from the dented metal side.

The metallic scent of blood filters into my nose and I push down the images that threaten to overpower my senses.

Marchetti's man peeks over the garbage bin, aims at my teammates, and fires before ducking back down. He doesn't notice how close I am to his side of the dumpster.

"Starling!" The word is strangled as it breaches Clarity's throat.

A body thumps to the ground.

My blood runs cold. This time I can't fight the visions. Vale sprawled on the ground. Julep trying to pry Clarity's hands off his throat. His lifeblood seeping between my sister's fingers. His eyes as his breath leaves him.

With a yell of fury I whip the gun out of the holster strapped to my thigh and shoot through the metal sheeting of the dumpster, dropping Marchetti's last remaining man with a shot to the chest. A groan slips between his lips as he slumps backward against the brick facade of the building.

Before Gavin can react, I'm ripping off my stilettos and vaulting out of the dumpster. I wince as my bare feet hit the dirty pavement, sending a jolt through my injured thigh. Sharp bits of glass dig into the soles of my feet, but I don't care.

At the end of the alley, Starling is flat on the ground on his back, arms and legs splayed like a starfish, his gun still clutched in his hand. His eyes are squeezed shut.

No.

Clarity is hunched over him, her hands moving over his chest. "Starling? Are you okay?"

I can't move. My feet are cemented to the ground. I can't take my eyes off my sister and Starling. He's not moving. Oh heart, he's not moving.

Lotus and Julep run up behind me, checking Marchetti's men with fingers pressed to the diminishing pulses of their veins. And behind them, Marchetti creeps toward us, steps hesitant. "Did it work?" he asks. "Is my family safe?"

Gavin stands and hauls himself out of the dumpster. "We've already moved them to a safe house. I'll take you to meet them now." He extends a hand toward the mobster. "Nicely done."

Marchetti sags in relief, pressing a hand to the brick wall to brace himself.

But my eyes are riveted to Starling.

Slowly, painfully, he sits up, unbuttoning his shirt to reveal a bullet proof vest. "That hurt a lot more than I expected."

I ragged exhale escapes me.

"It's a good thing you insisted we wear them, sis." Lotus pats me on the shoulder with one hand.

I nod, unable to look away from the boy on the ground. My entire body flushes as is brown eyes rise to lock on mine. Slowly he pushes to stand.

Seeing him upright loosens my feet, and I run to him, heart pounding. Throwing my arms around him, I press my lips to his. He wraps his arms around my waist and pulls me closer, breathing me in. Our hearts pound in unison as we squeeze each other tighter. It's the best kiss I've ever had, and I'm loathe to stop, but now really isn't the best time.

Licking my lips, I pull back. "Don't ever do that to me again."

The most luscious laugh rumbles from Starling's throat. "As you wish."

"It's pretty sexy when you say that."

Starling cocks an eyebrow. "Really? Shall I say it again?"

"Uh, guys? We really should get Marchetti to the safe house."

Elation builds in me as I turn to the rest of my team.

Starling slides his hand down the inside of my arm and takes my hand, sending delicious shivers over my skin.

I can't help the wide grin that parts my lips.

Royal steps up beside me, putting a hand on my shoulder. "Well done, all of you. I'm very proud."

My chin lifts at his praise, and as my gaze meets each of my teammates', I know we've earned it. Clarity, Lotus, Julep, Starling, Haru, and me, we've worked harder than ever. Pushed harder than I ever thought we'd be called upon to push. Done something the rest of the CIA hasn't been able to do for twenty years. We stopped Nexus from wreaking havoc on the agency's operatives around the world. We stopped a crime boss from terrorizing his community by putting him behind bars. And by helping Marchetti, we're breaking down la nostra società's hold on the Boston area.

Moving forward, every person on my team will be safe, and so will untold civilians both here and in Sicily. After this, there's nothing we can't do. We're ready for anything the CIA can throw at us.

And we did it together, as one. A family of spies.

Epilogue

It's been three months since Boston. Three months since Royal retired and left the Ivory Tower Spies under my leadership. Of course, we should probably change our crew name since we no longer live in the bunker under one of Charles Darnay's hotels. I tap my fingers on my thigh. Maybe we can come up with something later, after today's job.

"Earth to Loveday."

I blink rapidly as Lotus's voice breaks into my reverie. "What?"

"We'll be there in five minutes." He grips the plane's wheel with steady hands as we skim through the clouds.

"Thanks." Giving myself a mental shake, I peer out the window. The dawn sky is streaked with orange over the indigo hills. A hush falls over my team as we break into the light. The hum of the engine is the only sound in the silence of the fall morning.

I still can't believe that we're up here without Royal, but after everything that happened, Lotus was ready. My mouth lifts in a smile at the thought.

Behind the pilot's seat, Julep sits comfortably in her gear, talking to Clarity in a low voice. I'm so glad she passed up that job in LA to stay in D.C. with us.

I strain my ears but can't make out her words. My curiosity is peaked, but I don't have time to investigate. We're almost to the jump site.

A shiny black boot noses against my black tennis shoe, bidding for my attention.

I look up into Starling's eyes and smile.

He gives me a confident, easy grin in return. "You ready for this?"

"I was born ready."

His eyes spark. "Except for the part where you're supposed to land without ending up black and blue."

I bite my lip, holding back a laugh.

Starling's been teasing me about my uniformly disgraceful parachute landings since he first saw me jump a month ago. Really, he's not wrong. I've done over a hundred jumps and I still end up flat on my back, or with my face in the dirt.

In contrast, Starling glides into a smooth landing each and every time, a product of his years of military training. It's disgusting. And incredibly attractive.

"Remember what we practiced," he continues. "You can do this." Between us, his hand finds mine, and his thumb caresses my skin. My pulse speeds up.

It's been three months since we made it official, and yet his touch still sends a shiver through me. Being with Starling feels natural, like we were both made for this. There's a sense of contentment between us that I never felt with Vale.

"We're here," Lotus calls back. "You guys ready?"

I stand, checking in with each of my teammates. Once I confirm everyone is suited up and mentally prepared, I make my way to the front of the plane. "We're ready," I tell our eager pilot, reaching up to grip a handle on the plane's ceiling. "Open the door, will you?"

"Roger that." With a grin, he presses a button on the plane's console.

To my right, the door of the plane slides open, revealing the shiny green fields below us, illuminated by streaks of golden morning sun.

The short hairs on the back of my neck flutter in the wind, its icy cold like fingers raising goosebumps along my skin. Excitement courses through me as the time to jump nears.

"You're up," I call, pointing to Starling.

He marches to the plane door and sits, resting his feet on the sill outside the open hatch. "See you on the other side." He gives me a playful salute before flinging himself out of the plane. His body moves into a practiced, perfect formation for the freefall portion of the jump.

"Clarity," I say to my sister, meeting her large, brown eyes under perfectly arched eyebrows. "You're next."

She bites her lip, and nods.

Truthfully, parachuting has never been her favorite part of our job, so she avoids it whenever she can. Still, Royal suggested we all brush up from time to time, which is why we're an hour north of the city on this beautiful morning, taking turns nosediving out of his beloved aircraft. Honestly, I was surprised when he gave Lotus the keys to his own airplane, rather than finding us a plane with less sentimental value, but I didn't argue.

If Clarity is afraid, she buries the feeling. Her facial expression and movements are sure as she moves to stand beside me in front of the open hatch. "Here I go. One last jump," she says, putting a hand on my shoulder. Then she too sits on the sill before launching herself out into the blue.

Julep comes up beside me. "I'll bring up the rear," she

says, patting my arm with one hand. "You can do this. I know it."

"Thanks." I tip an imaginary hat to her before following in my sister's footsteps.

Breathing in the crisp air, I count down from five and shove myself away from the safety of the plane.

The freezing wind pummels my face and body, but I'm ready for it. I move into the proper form and begin counting the seconds. We're doing a twenty second freefall this morning, and keeping count is crucial.

The screen on my dad's watch blinks brightly as I descend, keeping track of my altitude and speed.

Streams of light fan out around me as the sun rises, making my vision go blindingly white. But I don't let it distract me from counting down. There are scant seconds to go until I deploy my chute.

Five

Four

Three

Two

I pull the cord and my chute springs out of my pack, billowing above me with an upward jerk of my pelvis. The thick harness straps cut into my skin in a familiar pinch, and my momentum slows. My equipment is functioning just as it should.

Gripping the toggles, I steer toward the designated landing zone.

Below me, I catch a glimpse of Starling touching down without even having to run out his remaining momentum. How does he do that?

I shake my head. Sometimes that guy is so good it's maddening. It's obvious why Royal recruited him to join our team.

Clarity hits the ground running, burning off the last of her speed as her parachute floats to the earth behind her. Starling is at her side in a moment, helping her unclip her gear before clearing the path for me to land.

I visualize the movements Starling and I talked about, getting ready for my own touch down. My jaw clenches in determination. Today is going to be the day I stick this landing, instead of eating a mouthful of dirt.

My body tenses as I approach the ground, but I will it to relax. I slow my speed and level out, preparing to run once I land.

The slick, grassy plain rises toward me, stretched out all around in an expanse of green.

Ready. Steady. Run!

I hit the ground and burst forward, legs pumping, propelled by the wind. My parachute billows out behind me as I run. I'm doing it. Adrenaline surges through me, and I let out a cheer. "I did it!" Flinging my arms in the air, I turn to my teammates. "Did you see that?" I can't help it; I'm beaming.

Clarity skims over the grass and throws her arms around me. "You nailed it!" she says, smiling. "Wait until we tell Dad."

Starling saunters up behind her, grinning at me over her head. "You were brilliant."

The moment is broken by a shout from above. "Incoming!"

We swivel to look upward, and not a second too soon.

Julep is gliding straight toward us, waving an arm to signal for us to move out of the way.

The three of us jump to the side as she buzzes over our heads and lands, skimming along the ground like she was taught. Her body is positioned just like a baseball player sliding into second as she tears through the grass.

Standing up, she brushes herself off. Her eyes are shining as she walks over to us. "What a rush."

"I'm coming in for a landing," Lotus says over our earbuds.

"See you in a few," I respond, turning back to get my chute. "Let's roll and go."

"Yes, ma'am," Starling says with a chuckle.

I roll my eyes, not so secretly loving it.

It takes us a couple minutes to pack up our chutes and tuck them under our arms. We'll check them over once we get back to our new base of operations.

"Let's get home," I say, slinging my arm around my sister's waist and pulling her close.

She smiles down at me, relieved to have completed her final parachute jump with our team, and puts an arm around my shoulder. "Ready when you are."

The four of us tromp across the grass, ready to start yet another unpredictable day.

"Think anyone will shoot at us today?" I quip.

At my side, Clarity shakes her head. "Talk about a quick way to kill the mood."

Julep busts up laughing, and the honky sound makes me crack up too.

"No, I think it'll be pretty uneventful," I say between giggles.

"I hope so, for Truly's sake."

Beside Julep, Starling's head bobs in agreement. Nothing like gunfire to break up a wedding.

Lotus pulls the van up to the street outside our new

headquarters, a three story brick townhouse on a corner near Seward Square. We had it fortified, of course, but from the outside the arched windows and fluttering curtains look perfectly normal. There's no evidence that the basement has been turned into command central for our elite group, or that the windows are ballistic glass.

"We've got an hour before we have to be at the church," I say as we climb out of the van. "Is that enough time for you?" I meet my sister's eyes, and she shrugs, eyes shining.

"I'll do my best."

"Come on, then." I run up the stairs to the front door, my fingers skimming over the wrought iron railing. Honestly, since she enrolled at her makeup and costume design school, she's been even more experimental than before and often comes home from class decked out as an otherworldly being. Last week, she came home from a class all done up as a female superhero with green skin and facial prosthetics.

Haru flings open the wood and glass front door to our new headquarters. "I'm so glad you're back. I have no idea what to wear to an American wedding." She's got several dresses on hangers in her grip, and holds them up for us to see. Baron tries to slip out between her feet, but Lotus scoops up the large cat and carries him back into the house, despite the feline's yowls of annoyance.

"Julep?" I ask over my shoulder.

"On it," she says, ushering Haru out of the hallway and back toward her room.

"Remember, one hour," I call as I pound up the stairs to my own room, the boys at my heels.

Bathed in the morning sun, the cathedral looks almost

otherworldly. Its towering spires and stained glass windows are beautiful.

Clarity pauses on the sidewalk, gawking up at the ancient structure. She'll never tire of seeing interesting architecture.

"It's amazing what people can do, isn't it?" she breathes.

I take her hand and pull her toward the side door, where the rest of our family is waiting.

Starling holds the door open for us as we rush inside the massive, dimly lit space. Above us, arches span the length of the room and pillars as big around as small cars rise from the floor all the way up to the ornate ceiling. Stained glass windows are set into the walls at regular intervals, their colored glass casting a blue glow over the interior.

We make our way up the side aisle toward the chapel.

Behind me, I can hear Haru chattering with her parents in Japanese.

A gold-plated gate of delicate scrolls hangs open, beckoning us into the Chapel of the Saints. Inside there's a marble altar with a golden figure of some ancient church father, and beneath it a wooden pedestal where the reverend will deliver the ceremony.

Royal is standing to one side, pacing back and forth in his black suit with an ivory shirt and champagne vest and tie. He sighs in relief when he sees us.

"Nervous, Dad?" Clarity asks as she glides over to him. "You forgot something." Pulling a boutonniere out of her purse, she fastens it to the lapel of his jacket before smoothing her hands over his shoulders. "You look handsome."

"Thank you."

The reverend sweeps into the room in his green and white robe, and sets his bible down on the pedestal. "If you'll take your places," he says with a friendly twinkle in his eyes.

Royal moves to stand beside the reverend, and the rest of us take our seats in the two rows of chairs that have been set up for the wedding.

"This is so exciting," Haru chirps from her seat behind mine.

"It is," Clarity responds, turning to smile at the girl and her parents.

On my other side, Starling takes my hand and gives it a light squeeze. I bump my shoulder into his before sitting up straight.

Nearby, a lone violin starts playing the wedding march.

"All rise."

We stand and turn to see Truly walking up the aisle toward us, her form swathed in a delicate off the shoulder sheath gown covered with silver and champagne lace. Her golden blond hair falls over her shoulders in loose curls and she carries a bouquet of white calla lilies in her hands. She smiles as her bright blue eyes meet my dad's.

My stomach flips at the intensity of their gaze. Holy mama they love each other. It's kind of inspiring, actually.

Truly reaches the pedestal, still beaming up at my dad.

The violin goes quiet as it hums on our periphery.

Leaning out, I retrieve Truly's bouquet so she can take my dad's hands, and slide back into my seat.

The reverend starts his message about the enduring quality of true love, and I can't help but glance down our row at Julep and Lotus, whose fingers are intertwined in Julep's lap. It's been fun watching them draw closer over the past few months, out of the shadows of Royal's ban on intra-squad relationships.

"Hey."

Speaking of intra-squad relationships.

I turn my eyes up to Starling's, and he leans down to

whisper in my ear. "I've been thinking about your new, no secrets policy, and there's something I've been wondering."

My stomach flips in anticipation. What could it be now? I rummage around in my head for secrets I may be keeping from him and come up empty. My brow furrows in confusion. "Yes?"

His breath tickles my ear as he speaks. "What's your real name?"

My skin warms at the question. It's about time I told him. It's only fair since I know his. Tilting my lips up toward his ear, I whisper my name, the name my mother gave me, to the boy who has laid claim on my heart.

When he hears it, his mouth widens into a grin. "That's perfect," he says. He squeezes my fingers, and we both return our focus to the front of the chapel, where my dad and Truly are about to say their vows.

Clarity is holding the rings in her lap, sparkling in their respective black velvet boxes.

My own mouth widens into a contented smile. Tomorrow we may be called upon to save the world from an as-yet unknown threat, but for now, being right here with my family, knowing we're capable of taking on whatever evil comes our way, Starling is right. This is perfect.

About the Author

Emily lives in sunny Southern California with her husband and daughters. She started writing in elementary school and continued writing in college, where she earned a degree in creative writing. She often gets ideas for stories from the lives of her friends and family. When she's not writing, she enjoys cuddling with her two dachshunds Nestlé and Kiefer, crocheting, watching television, and enjoying the sunshine with her daughters and their flock of backyard chickens.

To learn more about Emily, visit her website: www.emilykazmierski.com

CPSIA information can be obtained
at www.ICGtesting.com
Printed in the USA
BVHW031701130420
577501BV00001B/37